SHOBHA BO[illegible] ed Marathi writer. She ha[illegible]s and has published 18 b[illegible]e gone into over 30 edition[illegible]w keen to read her works [illegible]o English, Hindi, and Gu[illegible]t stories, and columns fo[illegible] like the *Maharashtra Times*, *Loksatta*, *Lokprabha*, *Maher*, *Kirloskar*, etc. She has also written dialogues for many popular Marathi TV serials like *Abhalmaya*, *Manasi*, *Oon Paaus*, and *Ardhangini*. In the last few years, personality profiles of people from various walks of life has become Shobha's forte. For this, she interacts closely with her subjects, understanding them in their social, familial, emotional, and economic settings. She has won many literary awards for her work, including the *Maharashtra State Award for Best Novel* in 1997, for *Saata Samudrapar*.

SATISH JOSHI graduated with a Bachelor's Degree in Electrical Engineering (1978) and a Master's in Computer Science (1980) from the Indian Institute of Technology (IIT), Mumbai. After graduation he worked in Tata Institute of Fundamental Research (TIFR) for three years. During his stint in TIFR he was involved in various technology development projects in areas such as Distributed Computing, Parallel Programming Languages and Systems etc. For the next 34 years till he retired in 2014 he worked for Patni Computer System which was later acquired by and became IGATE Global Solutions Ltd. During those 34 years, he led and managed teams delivering Engineering Solutions, IT solutions, providing IT infrastructure management and BPO services for a variety of business segments globally – primarily, Manufacturing, Hi-Tech Electronics, Automotive, Heavy Engineering and Life Sciences Industries. Prior to the acquisition of Patni by IGATE he has also been responsible in Patni for the CIO/CTO function and as the Head of Technology and Innovation responsible for incubating new technology driven service offerings for the company.

For more than two decades he co-edited and wrote a column about new developments in science and technology in every issue published in those two decades in Patni's quarterly in-house magazine first called *Bits&PCS* and later *FWD*.

NDRE is a celebrated and much publishe
s been writing for the last 25 year
ooks, many of them bestsellers that have
s. The non-Marathi reading world is no
and her books are being translated int
jarati. She has written articles, shor
prestigious publications like

7/1/2018

Dear Deepak.
Wish you and
all Khopkars
A Very Happy New Year
Shobhatai

THE SIXTH ELEMENT

SHOBHA BONDRE

SATISH JOSHI

Also by Shobha Bondre

Dhandha: How Gujaratis do Business (2013)
Mumbai's Dabbawalla : The Uncommon Story of the Common Man (2012)

THE SIXTH ELEMENT

SHOBHA BONDRE

SATISH JOSHI

Rumour
Books
India

www.rumourbooks.com

Rumour Books India
Plot. No 40, Sector 4, Panchkula, Haryana — 134 112

Sales Centres:
Chandigarh New Delhi Bangalore Mumbai
www.rumourbooks.com

First published Worldwide by Rumour Books India in 2017
First Edition: 2017

ISBN: 978-1-635-35346-4

Find out more about Rumour Books India at
www.rumourbooks

Typeset in Sabon by Satendra Singh, New Delhi

Printed and bound in India

This book is dedicated to the loving memories of our parents:
SHANTATAI *and* KAKA.
Shobha & Satish

सत्यमेव जयते

रक्षा मंत्री
भारत
MINISTER OF DEFENCE
INDIA

FOREWORD

When I thumbed through the pages of the book "The Sixth Element", I frowned with less excitability thinking it is yet another book on IT Industry. However, the initial pages drawn me slowly to read and later on grabbed my mind by engaging me in serious reading. The book is on the journey of an IT professional, in his quest to understand why and how computers have impaced our lives like no other human invention has done so far. On the whole the book is not mind-numbing but interesting to read while it throws light on the journey embarked by thousands of software engineers, in taking the Indian IT industry from infancy to global reckoning.

By virtue of my intimacy by sharing a same hostel at IIT Mumbai for five years with the author Satish Joshi, I knew him as a Nine-Pointer and avid cricketer but I now see a story teller in him- 'one more feather in his cap'. Satish and Shobha took me on this intriguing quest through anecdotes and experience right from Satish's first stumbling attempts to learn about computers during his IIT days, through his formative years in TIFR and later his participation in the remarkable development of the Indian IT industry. Early chapters of the book took me away to yester years that is almost 40 years back.

I wish Satish and Shobha all the best in their future endeavours for more literary feats.

Parrikar

(Manohar Parrikar)

Date: 26th August, 2016
Place: New Delhi

कार्यालय : 104, साउथ ब्लॉक, नई दिल्ली-110011, फोन : +91 11 23012286, +91 11 23019030 फैक्स : +91 11 23015403
Office : 104, South Block, New Delhi-110011, Ph. : +91 11 23012286, +91 11 23019030 Fax : +91 11 23015403

New Definitions of the New World

- The Six Elements:

  Earth, Water, Fire, Wind, Sky and Computer

- The Basic Necessities of Life:

  Food, Clothing, Shelter and Wi-Fi

Contents

Introduction

"The Sixth Element" is the story of modern-day addition of the sixth fundamental element—the Computer—and how the Homo sapiens are completely overwhelmed by this new element.

It is also the story of Satish Joshi, a witness and an occasional contributor to the journey of this new fangled gadget that evolved from just-a-curiosity stage to being as elemental in our lives as the five mythical elements—earth, fire, water, air and ether.

Having completed his master's degree in computer science from IIT Mumbai in 1980, Satish neither had any clue about what he was going to do with that degree nor any idea about how essentially computers were going to change the lives of people, including his own.

Satish worked for Patni Computer Systems, one of the early pioneers in the information technology (IT) industry in India, for more than 25 years. As the company's business expanded globally, he took on increasingly challenging projects, developing new technologies and eventually became an executive vice-president.

Patni Computer Systems was later acquired by IGATE and Satish continued to do what he loved the most—developing and deploying emerging technologies to create innovative solutions. He retired after three-and-a-half decades of this exciting journey.

Till the early eighties, computers and related technologies had no relevance in the every-day lives of ordinary people in India. It is hard to believe today, but this was the picture just about three-and-a-half decades ago.

The picture began to change rapidly as technology companies started taking roots in India, graduating from being traders of antiquated computing equipment to true engineers of solutions to increasingly complex industrial problems using computing and software technologies.

Practically in the blink of an eye (at least on the scale of geological time!), Indian IT Industry created a global brand. This was a watershed moment—perhaps the first instance ever of an Indian industrial endeavour competing on a global platform with the best in the world and beating them at their own game.

It was the hard work of many visionaries, such as F.C. Kohli, Narayan Murthy, Shiv Nadar, Azim Premjee and Naren Patni to name a few, who created the brand. Following in their footsteps were an increasing number of young technologists and engineers like Satish, with ambition in their eyes, conviction in their heart that they can be the best in the world with the drive to toil and succeed.

This book is also the story of this history that the Indian IT Industry created.

Generally, most people's view about IT and computers is rather narrow; only confined to those aspects of the industry or society where computers are directly visible as computers. However, a company like Amazon or Flipkart is as much an IT company as is IBM or TCS; even though Amazon or FlipKart make their money by selling books and gadgets and appliances like any retailer. Uber is as much an IT company as is Infosys even though Uber ostensibly runs taxis. A company like Genentech, which does research in genetics and designs innovative drugs by analysing chromosomes and genes, is at its core an IT company. Banks are fast transforming themselves into IT companies, as money is shedding its physical avatar of notes and coins and becoming virtual. The hands of computers which help make these kinds of businesses a reality are completely invisible.

Whether it is a matter of increasing milk production on a dairy farm in the UK or it is the challenge of providing medical advice to a patient on a ship thousands of miles away from the nearest shore, the invisible hand of computer has reached far corners of the world and beyond to provide help.

How far will this invisible hand reach? Only time will tell.

But consider this: when you were growing up, who was it that you were told to emulate?

In all likelihood, it was the bright boy in the neighbourhood who always stood first in his class, who was able to do arithmetic calculations faster than you, who was able to recite history better than you, who was able to fill in the blank: "Djibouti is the capital of ______"; who never made a mistake in his English grammar, who was the inter-school chess champion in the district.

Computers can do ALL of these tasks—the commonly accepted benchmarks of a bright "human" mind—better and faster than any human being who has ever lived on this earth. That does not mean computers have become more "intelligent" than us but it does mean that we need to reexamine all our definitions of what until now were deemed as quintessential human characteristics. Never before in the history of technological development has a resultant product caused such an upheaval in our definition of "humanness"!

"The Sixth Element" is also the story of that upheaval.

Shobha Bondre

CHAPTER ONE

Close Encounters of the "First" Kind

The Computer: The Sixth Element of Today's World

I still remember vividly the first time I saw a "computer". The year: 1974. The location: computer centre on the campus of IIT Mumbai. I was among several second-year engineering students who were waiting patiently in a queue outside the centre.

It was a momentous occasion—not very different from paying homage to a powerful God by visiting His temple and bowing before Him. The Computer was enshrined in a huge hall deep inside the centre behind two glass doors.

As in a temple, you had to leave your shoes outside to be allowed inside the outer hall. Like the others, I too, put aside my chappals and entered the holy place. Our next instruction was to stand with our hands behind our back (so that we did not inadvertently touch something in the room). I meekly followed the instruction and started looking around with curiosity. I peered inside, almost touching my nose to a floor-to-ceiling glass partition separating devotees like us from the inner sanctum and got my first glimpse of the glittering red, blue and green lights in the middle of a huge 7-foot-tall and several feet wide mighty machine perched on a pedestal in the sanctum sanctorum.

"So, this is what a computer looks like," I thought aloud.

Only the high priest, called the Computer Operator, had access to the deity itself and only the operator could communicate with the computer through a paper tape or stiff cardboard cards on which were punched a set of holes in complicated patterns.

To get your questions answered, you either had to learn the language of the God, such as Fortran or Cobol, or enlist the help of someone who had that knowledge.

It was akin to approaching a priest—with the complete knowledge of all the rituals to perform a puja—if you wanted the deity in the temple to answer your prayers.

"Do you have the punched cards?"

"Have you written your name and roll number on them?"… the brusque questions in a rough voice brought me out of trance. I put my hand through a tiny window and gave the set of punched cards tightly bound with a rubber band to the man who had asked the questions. This then was my first, "direct" encounter with the computer.

He took the cards I had given him, sat in front of a gadget that looked like a typewriter and started typing away on the keyboard. I watched him in awe for a few moments and then left the computer centre.

The next day, I was back in front of the small window to see if the program I had written on those cards was correct. After several trips to the computer centre and several corrections, I finally submitted the cards again and was at last successful in writing my very first computer program.

But at the time I still had absolutely no idea what the computer could be used for. Most of the people around me were not even aware of the existence of the computer. Although I saw it every day in IIT, it played no part whatsoever in my day-to-day life.

Fast forward to the year 2007, and how dramatically the picture had changed! It was another routine business trip to Japan. My Japanese friend Daiki and I were in a taxi, going for a meeting in Tokyo. Somehow or the other the conversation turned to how pervasive the presence of computers had become. He said, "Let's count the number of computers within our touching distance at this very minute, and gauge what they are doing."

Each of us had a laptop in our bags that we had kept in the middle seat between us. We had a cell phone each in our shirt pocket that contained a computer as powerful as the mighty 7-foot-tall machine that I had gone to pay my respects to thirty years ago. Daiki had a digital watch (powered by a tiny computer) on his wrist that was capable of synchronizing its time by receiving a satellite signal and which could tell the time in fifty different cities in the world.

The car we were sitting in had a navigation system powered by a computer that was receiving and interpreting the signal from GPS satellites.

Under the hood of the car were tiny computers that were determining how much fuel to inject in the combustion cylinders depending on the speed of the car and inclination of the road and were adjusting the tension in the suspension springs while taking fast turns. Computers were all around, underneath and in our pockets and we weren't even consciously aware of most of them.

This conversation with Daiki stayed at the back of my mind. Thirty years ago common folk had nothing to do with computers. Even though I had learned about computers in IIT, I had no clue then about what I was going to do with this knowledge about something so completely irrelevant to my everyday existence.

Today, three decades later, we wake up to a new day because of a cock-a-doodle-do sung by our mobile phone at a time determined by a tiny computer in it. Our breakfast is cooked to perfection by the computer inside the microwave oven. Yesterday's soiled clothes are thrown in the washing machine that determines the precise number of cycles needed to clean and dry them using a computer embedded inside. We rush to our offices using a car, bus or a train safely because of a signaling system which is driven by a computer to regulate the traffic. Upon reaching our offices we are deposited on our desired floors in the office building efficiently by the computer which controls the operations of the lifts in the building.

And, while performing all these daily chores, we don't spare even a moment to think about the invisible hand of the mighty computer which is the driving force behind all these things.

We have been surrounded by machines of all kinds for ages past and will be surrounded by machines in the time to come. None, however, has (or had in the past) the ability to touch our lives as pervasively and as intimately as the computers have done. That is a magic only computers can weave.

The spell of this magic is not confined only to the modern, technology-driven urban life. The technologies enabled by computers such as remote sensing are today scanning every square inch of the earth's surface or monitoring the smallest shifts in atmospheric conditions, through the constellations of satellites orbiting the earth. Remotest corners of the most inaccessible locales have come within the reach of the communication networks—radio, mobile phones and television.

As a result even the areas with no electricity, where people still go to a river to wash their clothes, can gain access to the news of the world, to forecasts providing warnings of impending natural calamities, agricultural advisories, banking services, distance learning and medical advice.

I am reminded of the legend of Waman, who, shedding his diminutive form, expanded to such a big size that he encircled the entire earth and pushed the evil Bali to the nether world in just three steps. Computers have similarly girdled our world like Waman in just three decades, but by going in the opposite direction, i.e., by shrinking in size.

How and when did this once-giant deity, enshrined in an inaccessible air-conditioned temple, escape unnoticed from its fortifications and became an essential part of our lives by assuming a microscopic but ubiquitous persona? Before anyone could say “eureka”, how did it enter our homes, offices, vehicles and even our pockets?

And when did it become an omnipresent, omniscient, omnipotent but benevolent sixth element?

To answer all these questions I must turn the clock back to the IIT Mumbai campus in 1973.

CHAPTER TWO

Love at First Byte

I entered IIT Powai campus in Mumbai in 1973 to pursue the B.Tech. programme in electrical engineering. At that time there was no separate programme offered by IIT leading to a B.Tech. degree in computer science.

In fact, there wasn't even a separate department of computer science. There was just a computer centre and a very active, enthusiastic bunch of young faculty members working hard to establish themselves on equal footing with all the "conventional" departments of engineering.

Anyway, at that time the subject "computer programming" was taught in the second year to the students of all engineering streams. Till then the only encounter with a computer, which I had experienced, had been with its many fanciful avatars described in science-fiction stories like Isaac Asimov's Multivac which in the story "The Last Question" reverses even the second law of Thermodynamics or Arthur Clarke's *Sentinel* (which later became famous because of the movie *2001 – A Space Odyssey*).

But the first time ever I saw a real computer, it was undoubtedly love at first byte!

And, as it happens in such situations, I was bowled over without really understanding why. Perhaps all that science-fiction reading had conditioned me to believe that one day all those miraculous feats of a computer described in books by Asimov, Clarke, Heinlein, and Silverberg would become a reality.

In the IIT library I came across serious periodicals, research papers and journals which while not quite confirming the fantastic deeds described by Asimov or

Clarke nevertheless described sufficiently interesting developments in computing to bolster my conviction that here was a product of our ingenuity that was capable of transforming every facet of industry and our very lives.

On the other hand, my immediate environment in India at that time was completely oblivious to the existence and potential impact of this fantastic machine.

The first computer that I saw in 1974 was called Minsk-II. It was made in Russia and was part of the equipment donated by the Russian government to India in 1967 while IIT Mumbai was being established. By world standards of that time this was a prehistoric dinosaur! One could only communicate with it using a paper tape with punched holes. It had a gigantic memory of 8 kilobytes! There was of course no monitor or any other device to show you what was happening inside. There was a large console with blinking lights and an array of switches. If you learned (after a lot of hard labour—which I didn't till well into my fifth year) to interpret the lights you could make a good guess about what the computer was doing at some point in time.

Even though Minsk-II belonged more to a museum of archaeological artifacts, it still functioned. It allowed one to learn the fundamentals of programming and perhaps because it was so primitive it provided an opportunity to really get to the gory innards of computing which a more modern device may have hidden from us. We just loved it!

Around the same time, or a little before I started learning programming in 1974, a new "powerful" computer called EC-1030 arrived in IIT. This was also Russian and was a copy of IBM 360. This sported a great convenience over Minsk-II; called "punched cards".

One could communicate with EC-1030 using a deck of cards with holes punched to represent your program instead of the paper tape of Minsk-II. With the paper tape the problem was that even if you punched one wrong character on the tape, the whole tape containing hundreds of lines of your program had to be thrown away. With the deck of cards one needed to replace just that one wrongly punched card. Phew! That was several hours of labour and late nights saved.

However, I didn't really mind those late nights. This was a fantastic new toy and the fulfilment experienced was like no other—when the results printed out on paper looked correct after several nights of labour. It did not matter whether those results had any practical value.

For example, one of the early projects as a part of my programming course consisted of writing a program to print out hostel mess bills. I hounded the mess manager to learn how he prepared the bills manually. I translated all that into a program and spent sleepless nights on the card punching machines to prepare my program. After several days of ironing out the errors when finally the printed results matched our three-month-old mess bill the exhilaration was no less than what Tenzing Norgay would have experienced after arriving at the top of Mount Everest.

It didn't matter when a hostel mate with a more practical bent of mind remarked that the mess manager had taken only two days to do the same thing!

How long did it take to print the mess bills wasn't the pertinent question. The real question was—what did I learn out of this exercise? Because it was clear that while it may have taken weeks (and not two days) to get the mess bills printed correctly the first time, from then on it was going to take only hours (or even minutes) to do so on every subsequent occasion.

During all this time of learning the basics of programming, the computer to me was still a complicated and sophisticated "calculating" device. The first inkling that computing is something much more than calculating started dawning on me when I took a course called Boolean algebra in my second year.

The only reason I registered for this course was its strange name.

This was a course offered by the mathematics department available as 'no-credit' (i.e. even if you did well in the course it did not reflect in your performance) elective to all students. Superficially it seemed to have no relation to either electrical engineering (which is what I was formally a student of) or computers (which is what had captured my fancy). I had no idea then about how fundamentally this was going to start altering my perception about computers.

Boolean algebra defines a rigorous mathematical formulation of the laws of logic (among other things). And therefore, in principle, it can be applied to represent any logical argument. Such arguments could then be translated into a computer program, i.e., wherever we employ logic to arrive at a rational decision, in theory an appropriate computer program could be written to do the same thing.

This seemed like such a mind boggling, powerful concept because this wasn't number crunching. In fact there are no numbers in Boolean algebra; there are only statements, rules of inference and conclusions that are guaranteed to be correct if all the rules are followed.

I didn't fully comprehend the implication of this at that time but undoubtedly this provided impetus to try and unravel the complicated puzzle of computers and computing. And, I was fortunate to run into the right guru at the right time—Prof. Isaac.

I had not met anybody like the amazing Prof. Isaac. He was like a cyclone, sweeping everything and everybody who came in his path. He was completely driven by his own total fascination with computers and had the power to infect anybody within ten miles of him with his energy and enthusiasm for the subject.

He had an instant connect with his students (and even with those who were "formally" not his students);

he would do anything, be available at any time of day or night to teach if you wanted to really learn something new.

He had the foresight and vision to recognize how the world was going to get transformed by the power of computer. He had seen how the world outside India was galloping to use this new technology and harboured a burning desire to create the environment to learn about and develop this new field in IIT.

He had struggled tirelessly in the face of hidebound bureaucracy, resistance arising out of lack of foresight and hardened arteries of the old guard, to lay the foundation of a Department of Computer Science.

It had not yet happened when I entered IIT but the seeds were already sown by him and other faculty members who were equally super-charged by his enthusiasm. The computer centre was set up on the ground floor of the mathematics department. Minsk-II had arrived and was already being superseded by EC-1030.

In 1974 when I started my first programming course, as luck would have it, Prof. Isaac conducted that course. His passion was infectious. He would come into the classroom on a run and literally take a small leap on the platform. He would spellbind us for the next hour and then jump down from the platform and sprint away for his next engagement. If we needed to ask him something after the class and did not find him in his office in the computer centre, we would go running around all over the campus and find him rushing like the wind somewhere. We would also then start jogging alongside and talk. And the strange thing was that he who literally sprinted everywhere probably because he didn't like to waste even a second in a leisurely walk, used to have all the time in the world to spend with his students to make sure all their questions were answered and difficulties addressed.

He lent me a book once to read and told me to return it after four days. I didn't find him in his office in the evening. So I went to his house. I entered his room and my jaw dropped like Alibaba's must have after entering the cave of treasures. Every wall of his room was covered with shelves overloaded with books. He took the book I had come to return, climbed over a stool and inserted the book in its designated slot. While we were talking, repeatedly he was unerringly pulling out the exact book, which contained some matter relevant to what we were talking about. Among those hundreds of books he knew exactly where each book was located and what it contained.

I had decided right then that some day when I could afford it, I would have a room in my house exactly like his with the walls covered with books. And I did create such a room—that was easy. The difficult part was to be able to remember the exact contents and the exact location of each of those books. I don't think I have quite got the second part yet. Prof. Isaac was undeniably instrumental in getting me completely fascinated by computers and, more than that, the cause to make me start looking beyond just the little I learned in his course on computer programming. However, the person who got me literally wedded to computers, and opened the door to a lifelong career was someone else—Prof. Dhamdhere.

I was a third-year student in the electrical engineering department. The Electrical Engineering Student's Association (EESA) had arranged a series of talks for all of us. In the fourth and fifth year we had the freedom to choose a certain number of elective courses from amongst a large number of options, which were, till then, only curious names to us.

In order to help us make knowledgeable choices, EESA had arranged for a number of professors to come and talk to us about each of these elective courses on offer. Each such talk used to be just about fifteen minutes.

Prof. Dhamdhere came to talk about "Systems Programming" in particular but also spoke about computer science in general.

Until then I had gathered fragments of apparently disconnected pieces of information. I had learned programming in the course taken by Prof. Isaac, I had learned about Boolean algebra with some half-baked notion that this had something to do with computing, I had also read a little bit about Shannon's Information Theory—while being intrigued by it, I had understood little of its implications.

Those fifteen minutes of utterly fascinating talk made all these little pieces of jigsaw fall into place and opened a new window, through which glimpses of the enchanting world of computing beyond "calculations" were fleetingly visible.

That talk was a demonstration of the phrase "crystal-clear thinking"; so lucid was his description of this strange new world. That was the moment of decision. I decided to sign up for all the computer science related electives, which I was allowed to in the fourth and the fifth year. I had made up my mind to seize this opportunity to enter the world that Prof. Dhamdhere had shown us through this small window of his fifteen-minute talk.

At that time, of course, I had no idea where this decision was going to take me. I had no idea that something called IT industry was slated to spring forth in India in a short period of time and that I was going to get married to it for life.

CHAPTER THREE

More Than Meets the Eye

Inspired by Prof. Dhamdhere's talk, I signed up for all the electives available related to computing for my fourth and fifth year. Although some of these were mandatory, core courses for the recently started full master's programme in computer science, B.Tech. students were allowed to register for them. I could not foresee how this was to lead me to a major conflict with the IIT officialdom later.

Five or six other fellow students, equally enamoured by this new area, had also taken the plunge.

I was, in fact, cautioned by one of our electrical-engineering faculty members that this choice would make me less of an electrical engineer compared to my other classmates and harm my prospects of landing a good job!

These electives consisting of Discrete mathematics (the mathematical foundations of the Theory of Computing), Computing Architecture, Systems Programming (Prof. Dhamdhere's Course) etc., set me on the journey from "hey, this is a fascinating new gadget" to "this is how this new engineering marvel is constructed".

And, during the course of this journey, the two concepts around which my professional life was to revolve, viz. computing and information, started becoming clearer and clearer.

Around this time, there was a show by Shakuntala Devi in our convocation hall. The advertisement for the show had created considerable buzz around the campus because it said, "Famous mathematician Shakuntala Devi who can compute faster than the fastest computer in the world will be giving a lecture/demonstration of her amazing skills."

As the show progressed Shakuntala Devi absolutely dazzled the audience by providing answers instantly to complex calculations involving really large numbers—division and multiplication of twenty-three-digit numbers, square roots and cube roots of eighteen-digit numbers, correctly identifying the day of the week it was on a date twenty-five years in the past and so on.

Soon, however, it started becoming apparent that she was no "mathematician" in the sense that we understood the word. A mathematician to us was someone like Pythagoras or Euler or Reimann or Kurt Gödel or Alan Turing who discovered and formally proved new "truths".

What was being displayed on the stage was an amazing skill to perform arithmetic calculations without using any tools, but it wasn't "mathematics".

When some student got up and asked a question related to solutions of systems of differential equations, she admitted that she didn't have the answer. It was a very basic question. The kind that a student who has just started learning the subject may ask based on quite cursory knowledge.

After the show, for the next week or so the dominant topic that consumed all my hostel mates was whether there exist techniques which when learned properly and practised hard enough can enable anyone to emulate what we saw on stage. Some of my friends pored over books in the library, some of them were seen furiously scribbling on paper and sometimes on the walls of their rooms.

It wasn't uncommon to find in the early morning, sitting at the table for breakfast in the mess while the cobwebs of sleep were still occluding my mind, my neighbour suddenly turning and asking, "Give me two seventeen-digit numbers and I will multiply and tell you the answer."

Some of us who were rather more "learned" about computers had become familiar with the binary number system. Very soon we discovered that indeed with a bit of practice we could do some of the simpler tricks we had seen Shakuntala Devi perform, as long as the numbers were written in binary form.

Clearly then whatever amazing feats we had seen on the stage that day during the show were nothing beyond what a computer could do. Whether she could do these any faster than the fastest computer then known, as it was advertised, was also somewhat questionable.

Nowhere had anyone published the specific method used to measure, compare and thereby declare that the computer was indeed defeated by her in this contest.

Given what we were learning about the technological advances being made, it was apparent that in the near future the power of computers to do these kinds of calculations would increase at such a rate that no human—Shakuntala Devi's claims notwithstanding—will be able to match it.

There was however a deeper question here (the answer to which I was destined to continue to seek).

Could a computer do something more than arithmetic operations? Could it be programmed to answer truly mathematical questions of the kind which had stumped Shakuntala Devi?

Shakuntala Devi's programme was one of those incidences that contributed to my understanding of the largely uncharted world of computing, but so were the lectures, lab projects and field trips.

Field trips used to be fun. The ostensible purpose of course was educational but it was an equally welcome diversion from the pressures of campus life. A lot of Machiavellian plotting used to go on in the background to kill many birds with one stone—like slipping out for a movie at Regal after a visit to Videsh Sanchar Nigam building.

For some of us in the class somewhat more committed to computing technology, this plotting was also necessary to include locations of special interest to us because being students of electrical engineering these trips were organized by the electrical engineering department and would generally select organizations or businesses directly related to electrical engineering.

We had to use subtle creativity to make sure places like Videsh Sanchar Nigam or Bhabha Atomic Research Centre (BARC) or Tata Institute of Fundamental Research (TIFR) were included. All these organizations had computers much more advanced than the archaic Minsk-II or EC-1030 on our campus. And the things they were doing with this modern technology in their research, in telecommunications, in astronomy was mind boggling.

A trip to Ooty was an example of such successful manoeuvering. Who wouldn't want to escape the heat and oppressive humidity of Mumbai in summer and go to a beautiful, cool place in the mountains like Ooty, especially if it could be sponsored by someone!

We discovered that near Ooty was a giant radio telescope, then one of the largest in the world. We finagled the permission to visit it. While travelling there all the talk and focus was on what we were going to do in Ooty. The visit to the radio telescope was just that necessary evil to be suffered in the larger interest of some great days in Ooty.

Having visited that Radio Astronomy centre however, we were dazzled by what we saw there—designed and constructed completely indigenously, it was a marvel of technology and at its heart was some of the most sophisticated computing technology driving its operations.

Soon after that field trip to Ooty, I had an important decision to make. It was the time to choose my final-year project; something which I would be working on all through the fifth year and which represented almost half the weightage for determining my final-year grades.

As usual a list was displayed on the notice board containing the names of the projects and faculty members who would be the guides for these projects. None of these listed projects sounded very "appetizing". Since this was an electrical engineering department list, most of the projects were about topics in core electrical engineering—something I had already turned my back on.

Just about then my friend Vikas Phatak and I got talking to Prof. Bhavsar. At that time Prof. Bhavsar was working with a team from BARC on an interesting application for cardiac monitoring.

He suddenly said, "Guys, I have an idea which may interest you and solve your problem of finding something exciting to do in your final-year project."

We were, of course, all ears.

He said, "Do you know what an Electrocardiogram is? Have you ever seen an ECG monitor? The project I am talking about is related to the ECG."

We certainly hadn't seen an ECG monitor until then nor were we sure why a professor who taught computer science subjects was telling two students of electrical engineering about some equipment which a doctor uses.

We wanted to do a project which had something to do with computers and failing that at least a run-of-the-mill electrical-engineering project. We were not medical students intending to be doctors!

Our confusion must have turned our faces into large question marks because he laughed and said, "Look, the wave which you see on a printed ECG or which is displayed continuously on a monitor contains information about the heart, its rhythm and its state of health. When the wave starts departing from its normal pattern it indicates that something is wrong.

"Usually a nurse is continuously looking at the monitor connected to a critical patient and when something abnormal is seen the nurse goes running to fetch a doctor who then interprets the pattern and figures out what, if anything, may have gone wrong with the patient.

"The project I have in mind will involve developing a system to automate this whole process—a system to capture all this information contained in the ECG, analyse the waveform and interpret it to draw conclusions about the condition of the patient's heart just as a doctor would do.

"Of course this is ambitious and nobody knows what kind of accuracy can be achieved. So initially we will focus only on being able to draw conclusions about only a small set of rhythm disorders (Arrhythmia)."

This was something mind boggling—this was a blow to my conception of the computer-as-a-calculating machine to calculate students' mess bills or payrolls. Here was something that would touch a person's very life directly and make a difference perhaps between life and death through the power of computing technology.

While the grand vision Prof. Bhavsar outlined for us was enthralling, we were still not clear about what we were to do in our project. Prof. Bhavsar clarified that.

"The two of you have to design the system, which will capture the ECG signal from the ECG machine and develop the programs that will analyse the captured signal to draw conclusions about a small set of specific arrhythmic conditions. We are going to use the latest microprocessor technology to design a compact and truly portable system."

This was sounding better and better. "Microprocessor technology" was the latest development, which was making waves in the world of computing at that time. Microprocessors, in a 2.5-cm-long and 1-cm-wide chip, were reputed to pack more computing power than our beloved Minsk-II.

Although we had read some exciting articles about it, we had never seen one— even in the whole IIT only a few had actually played with one. This was just the first glimpse of how the computer was going to shrink in size but expand in power.

"So what do you think? Want to accept this challenge?" Prof. Bhavsar asked.

It sounded like a purely rhetorical question. Of course, we were going to take this challenge.

"Okay then. Although this topic is not on the list of projects published by the department, I will get it included and I will be your guide for this project," he said. I wanted to kiss the ground he was walking on.

Vikas and I went back and had a small celebration—we feasted on a pastry in the hostel canteen!

We had to start from learning how to spell "electrocardiogram"!

We started hounding the doctors in the campus hospital—to get hold of old ECG records of past patients, to ask what the doctor sees in those faint squiggles and curves on graph papers.

We combed the library to find material to educate ourselves on techniques to analyse signals and recognize meaningful patterns in these obscure lines.

The results of this analysis and the extracted patterns had to be used to draw medically relevant conclusions—we needed help from relevant medical experts.

Everything was new, everything was exciting and fascinating, everything needed new questions to be answered—what kind of sensors are required to capture the ECG? How to store the captured signal? How to process it fast enough so that the analysis was complete before the next wave arrived?

Underneath all of this work was the realisation that this was also a vindication of the several albeit disconnected threads of thought at the back of my mind.

These threads were generated by the exposure to Boolean algebra, information theory, Shakuntala Devi's programme and so on, which had raised unanswered questions about the scope of computing technology.

This project was also a reconfirmation of the choice I had made when deciding on what electives to take and what area to pursue for further studies. I decided to continue my studies at IIT and enter the M.Tech. programme in computer science, which had been started in IIT very recently.

This was my fifth and last year of graduation and the campus was abuzz with recruitment activities; every day some company would hold interviews for prospective employees on the campus and many of my classmates would be seen rushing from one interview to the next. There would be heated discussions at the mess table about who was paying what and which company was better than the other—voices would be raised, somebody's sanity would be questioned.

I had little interest in all of this since I had decided to continue and complete M.Tech. But the atmosphere was contagious and purely out of curiosity I too went and appeared for a few interviews. Perhaps there was a bit of fear at the back of my mind that if, for some reason, I couldn't make it through the M.Tech. entrance examination, I might look like a fool.

I completed B.Tech. in electrical engineering with a CPI of 8.89 (out of 10) and waited for the first semester of M.Tech. to start.

A small but interesting incidence happened during the selection process for entering the M.Tech. programme. The selection process consisted of a written test and an interview by a panel of faculty members. Since I was an electrical engineering student but had applied for M.Tech. in computer science, my interview panel had professors from electrical engineering and as luck would have it, one of them was my B.Tech. guide Prof. Bhavsar.

One of the electrical-engineering professors asked me, "What were your fourth and fifth year electives?" I rattled off the list. On hearing the names, he, with a distressed look as if he had run into a disloyal renegade, told me, "I don't want to ask you anything" and turned to Prof. Bhavsar and said, "Go ahead, you decide"!

CHAPTER FOUR

Calculation vs. Computation

As the fresh semester started, I discovered that out of the mandatory courses for the first-year M.Tech. students, I had already completed three core courses during my B.Tech. stint. This had happened because during my fourth and fifth year I had chosen all the computer science related electives and three of these were actually M.Tech.-level courses, which B.Tech. students like me were allowed to take. My friend Anil Mankar was also in the same boat.

Doing the same courses a second time, taught by the same professors, especially when I had scored an 'A' grade in all of them, was a waste of time. I could have spent that time more gainfully by signing up for some other elective courses.

Anil and I went to the administrative office to talk to them about this. We told them that we were B.Tech. students of the same institute and had successfully completed these three M.Tech. courses in our final year of B.Tech. Therefore, we would like an exemption from these and be allowed to register for three other subjects.

This was my first experience of dealing with bureaucracy of any kind and it was like hitting a wall. Logic and common sense didn't matter. Rules were rules and were immutable. The irony in the blind enforcement of rules in this "great" institute of learning, resulting in us not learning anything new, was, of course, beyond their ability to understand.

We were told, "What you have learnt and where you have learnt it does not matter. You are students of M.Tech. computer science. These are mandatory courses for first-year students of M.Tech. computer science and you have to register for them. Otherwise later on you will not be allowed to register for the advanced courses in the same subjects for which these are prerequisites."

While the administrative office refused to budge, we kept going there every day for weeks; reasoning, arguing, quarrelling but nothing seemed to work.

Finally, the story of our recalcitrant behaviour reached Prof. Isaac, the head of the department then. We thought this was good, we loved Prof. Isaac and thought at least now we would get a rational hearing. But there was a surprise waiting for us. It was unlike the Prof. Isaac we knew—till today I don't know what happened that day and why he wouldn't even allow us to speak. His verdict was immutable: "Do as you are told and go attend your lectures."

Dejected we went back prepared to waste a substantial amount of time in the first semester. We went to the classroom for a lecture on systems programming by Prof. Dhamdhere. When he saw us, he asked, "What are you doing in this class? You did this elective last year. Are you just planning to goof off and take it easy by doing the same course again?"

We told him the whole story. Sometimes Prof. Dhamdhere could be as quick tempered as he was brilliant. He quite categorically told us, "I don't want to see your faces in this class. Go and sign up for subjects you haven't done before."

"But sir, they wouldn't let us," we said.

"That is not your problem, I will sort it out, you do as you are told and sign up for some other course you would like to learn," he replied.

Once again we were directed to "do as you are told" but what a difference between the implications of the two "do as you are told" statements!

And, sort it out he did! He somehow seemed to have convinced Prof. Isaac and the administrative office. We were allowed to drop out of these three courses under contention and were allowed to sign up for other courses and I was able to do advanced courses in signal processing and theory of computation.

The remaining two years of M.Tech. were a breeze. Every day was a day of some new discovery. Every day was a day of getting closer to answers to the questions about the nature of computing and the power of computers that had been growing at a fast pace since the time I learned about Boolean algebra.

Boolean algebra showed that logical arguments can be represented by symbols and simple but precise rules can be defined to manipulate these symbols. Logically correct conclusions could be arrived at without knowing or paying attention to the actual meaning of those symbols as long as the rules were followed faithfully. Alan Turing's abstract computing machine showed how this process of symbol manipulation could be done mechanically by a machine as well as it could be done by a human being.

The symbols could represent numbers, they could represent letters and words, they could represent pictures or fragments of pictures, they could represent heart beats (as they did in my B.Tech. project which I talked about earlier), and they could represent sounds or fragments of sounds—practically anything.

As long as a consistent set of rules to manipulate those symbols could be defined, a computer program could be constructed to derive correct conclusions using these rules.

If the symbols represented numbers you would have a computer-as-a-calculating-machine. If they represented words and phrases you would have a computer-as-a-grammar-checker. If they represented geographical features of the terrain around you, you would have computer-as-a-navigation-guide. The possibilities were limitless—at least in theory. In practice, making a computer do all these complex tasks needed some really hard problems to be solved. But that is precisely where people like me had a role to play.

By now my second year of M.Tech. was drawing to a close, my M.Tech. project was nearing completion and had resulted in getting, along with my guide Prof. Dhamd here, two research papers published in reputed international journals.

Meanwhile, the usual campus recruitment frenzy had begun and companies started visiting the campus to gobble up prospective employees. I had no reason to appear for any interview, even for fun, because I had already signed up to join Tata Institute of Fundamental Research (TIFR) and work there for three years since they had also sponsored my M.Tech. studies.

The final examination was looming; a bit of anxiety and impatience had started setting in. I had spent seven long years on the IIT campus and while that period was most fulfilling I was now looking forward to new experiences.

Having completed M.Tech. with a CPI of 10, I eagerly stepped into the new world outside the campus. This was potentially as disconcerting a transition as the upheaval I had experienced when I left the protected cocoon of my home and entered the IIT campus.

CHAPTER FIVE

It's a Mad Mad Mad Mad World

The story of someone who has graduated from an IIT cannot be considered complete without including an account of the campus life. The lessons learned from the life on campus are as profound as the formal education one receives there.

For most of the 18- or 19-year-old kids who arrive on the campus, it is their first brush with the hard knocks of the real world outside the cocoon built by their parents.

Their self-esteem takes the first blow. Almost every one of them is conditioned to believe that he is the most precocious, the smartest and the most intelligent bloke around because almost always he has, in fact, been the most decorated student from his respective school, college and town.

After landing on the campus they soon realize that everyone around them has gone through the same brutally tough entrance examination and has been *the* numero uno in their respective ponds. Every one of them is as bright, as smart if not brighter and smarter as they have believed themselves to be. In no time at all, inflated egos shrink in size, illusions of superiority shatter and the realization starts setting in that they are not that special after all.

In the aftermath of this reality check, it isn't easy to land on your feet and figure out how to find your individual station. I too went through this purgatorial passage. I saw kids all around me who could quite clearly outscore me in any academic pursuit.

The hardest part was accepting this reality. I had to condition myself to evaluate my self-worth based on what I did and not on whatever somebody else accomplished.

I had to train myself to concentrate on what I enjoyed learning and spending my time on and to stay focused on doing the best that I could.

Like me, most kids around me learned to make peace with their individual realities, figured out their own paths to create an identity for themselves amongst their peers. However, the spectrum of responses to these hard knocks to their hitherto secure perches on their pinnacles was as wide as their shapes and sizes.

Some of them responded with resignation. They decided that no matter how hard they worked, there wasn't the smallest hope that they will ever again be the apple of their teacher's eye. Their reaction was: "Why then spend sleepless nights worrying about topping tests, exams and grades? Let us savour the moment, enjoy the campus. Living on the campus provides plenty of avenues to manage a carefree existence shielded from the pressure to perform from parents and neighbours. Let us work just enough to scrape through. So what if we get Ds in all subjects? There is an IIT degree waiting at the end of five years anyway, and with that stamp of credibility on the forehead, options would be available to make a living".

Some of them refused to accept that they cannot score as much as their peers and cannot be always at the top of the class as they were used to being earlier in life. These people spent their entire time cooped up in their rooms furiously trying to absorb every word on every page of every text book they could lay their hands on. These people were only occasionally seen outside their rooms—perhaps while wolfing down their breakfast with an open book in one hand before rushing to the library to borrow more books, or perhaps while rushing to their classes with a frown on their face at the ruckus that the rest of us were creating in the mess hall.

Some others responded with abject surrender. They burnt their books, hardly ever saw the inside of the classroom or laboratories and focused on finding more and more creative ways of whiling away their time. They appeared for examination if they had nothing better to do on a given day. Didn't care whether they passed or didn't.

Whatever course everyone adopted, most managed to stay afloat and came out of this trying period pretty much unscathed. A very small number however weren't so lucky. They just broke under the pressure.

One of them was someone I had grown quite close to in the first few months after I entered the campus. And it was heartbreaking to see him completely destroy himself with drugs. What led to his addiction and eventually ending his own life? Whether it was the competitive pressure or the inability to recalibrate his aspirations with respect to the harsh reality which he found himself in, I could never figure out.

Despite all these travails and tribulations, life on the IIT campus was without question absolutely exhilarating. Suddenly I found myself in an environment where the constraints of social norms, rules and regulations didn't have to be strictly obeyed. The watchful and often intimidating eye of a loving parent or a stern school teacher wasn't burning a hole in the back of my neck as it used to. Leaving aside the six or seven hours, which bound me to the classroom or labs, the remaining hours of the day were mine to spend pretty much as I pleased and the avenues to do so were numerous.

There was a movie club which screened movies every week. There was a music circle if you were so inclined. There was an active, organized trekking club officially sponsored by the students' gymkhana and several unorganized, ad-hoc trekking groups. There was a photography club with a darkroom fully equipped with the required gadgets. There were volleyball and badminton courts, hockey and football grounds and a cricket pitch. If you didn't feel like going out in the hot sun, you could sit in your room, gather a few others who had nothing else to do and play bridge or carom or chess.

And if you were bored with all these, all you had to do was jump over the hostel boundary wall and go for an idle stroll in the jungle (was still a jungle behind the hostel in those days) or climb to the top of the hill which provided a breathtaking view of Powai and Vihar lakes and the IIT campus.

With the pristine waters of the lakes so close, the temptation to treat them as private swimming pools was obviously unavoidable. Powai, however, was known to harbour crocodiles and even in the devil-may-care state of mind, I think we retained enough sanity to not risk swimming in Powai.

Vihar Lake held no such threats. Of course, there was one small problem. The lake supplied water to the city and swimming in it was not legal. However, all the officialdom responsible for enforcing the law resided on the opposite side of the lake. This then was definitely a risk worth taking—or so we used to think and most of the times our idea worked.

Once in a while though a conscientious security guard would visit our side of the lake and capture a bunch of kids red-handed (or more accurately "wet undied")!

These unfortunate souls would then be driven in a jeep to the Vikhroli police station. Fortunately, the police there were an enlightened lot. They would shout and threaten these captives with dire consequences, if caught again, before letting them go.

As a result, it wasn't an unusual sight to occasionally see students in wet underwear, shivering, entering the campus gates and hightailing it to their hostels.

One day my friend Sandeep thought of a new trick. He appropriated empty kerosene cans from our mess and tied them together to create a raft. Next afternoon this wonderful feat of our engineering, which all of us were feeling very proud of, was launched with a lot of fanfare in the lake. Sandeep and a few others climbed atop to sail to the other end of the lake with nary a thought about the crocodiles in the lake that may have resented this invasion of their territory.

Such prudence was alien to us in those days given our age and the atmosphere on the campus. If some idea looked crazy enough and by and large didn't look like it will harm anyone except perhaps ourselves, it would just get pursued till the very end.

There was no telling where and when this madness would strike next.

It was some holiday on the campus and there was absolutely nothing to do in the afternoon. We decided to play cricket in the open space behind our hostel wing. Ramesh Chouhan who used to live two rooms down the corridor was the only one missing. So somebody knocked on his door and he was gruffly told, "Go away you SXX XX X XXXXX! Don't bother me, I am going to take a nap."

"Hey what the XXXX, who the XXXX does he think he is?"

We had to do something to retaliate. So we picked up Ramesh's bicycle, parked royally in front of his room, and gave it an elevated spot—high up on a branch of the tree behind the hostel.

We were all very proud of our handiwork. Of course, it had taken us all afternoon and hadn't been able to play any cricket, but that was not the point—the time was spent doing something interesting and entertaining, and *that* was the important thing. In the evening when we proudly invited Ramesh to witness our feat, he didn't know what to do.

For three days the bicycle was hanging on the branch—everybody from every other hostel came to admire this great new spectacle, which was also photographed and published in the Gymkhana newsletter. It, of course, took much more effort, a few scraped, bloody knees and elbows and one sprained wrist to bring the bicycle down without any damage done to it.

There is no dearth of these kind of anecdotes. There was that night I remember when a power outage plunged the whole campus suddenly in darkness. This was late, about 11 p.m. or so, the normal time when most people start thinking of putting in an hour or two of studies—especially since the end-semester exams were just round the corner.

It was impossible to sleep with the heat and swarms of mosquitoes desirous of getting cozy with us. Everybody gathered in the corridors. Usually, such times led to somebody coming up with some interesting lark to while away the time till the power came back. But that night all that creativity also seemed to have dried up.

So my friend Thomas and I decided we had to do something to make life a little bit more interesting for all of us. We picked up a book each and went down to the road next to the hostel wall. The street lights on the road were still on. We sat down under a street lamp pretending to be absorbed in our studies. We, of course, had no intention of actually studying under the street light (notwithstanding all the stories of all those great people who had become great and famous *because* they had been wise enough to study under a street light!).

However, we were sure this act of ours was going to instigate a riot of some sort in the hostel. We had also chosen our spot very carefully—not so close that something thrown from the hostel terrace or corridor would reach us but not so far that nobody could see us.

As expected, we were soon noticed and a crowd gathered on the hostel terrace and the corridor nearest to us. Soon buckets of water got chucked towards us but besides the road next to us getting wet and few splashes reaching our feet nothing happened. So instead of water, all manner of curses started getting chucked at us.

However, this was a game we could play too—so we stood up being careful to maintain our strategic position outside the range of any physical missiles and hurled choicest curses from our stock at them at the top of our voices. Aha! This was finally turning into an endeavour worthy of the trouble Thomas and I had taken. The "gaali" fight continued for some time with ever-increasing vigour and creativity but ended inconclusively when the power suddenly came back. So we picked up our books and walked calmly back to our rooms to sleep—content in the thought that we managed to create for everyone an interesting diversion for an hour or two.

I spent seven years in IIT and Hostel No. 4 and it would take a whole book to recount all the stories spanning those precious years. In fact, a book called *Madhouse: True Stories of the Inmates of Hostel 4, IIT-B* has already been written by a bunch of my friends from those days.

Obviously, life on the campus was much more than only these shenanigans. We were there in the first place to learn engineering and technology. In a way, perhaps this absolutely unfettered life was the safety valve to let off the pressures of our academic pursuits. This was the spicy stimulant needed to rejuvenate what would otherwise have been an insipid life full of tasteless hostel food, long lectures, intimidating quizzes and examinations.

When I look back now, many a time, I wonder what made us gallop unheeded and reckless like a horse holding the bit in its mouth. I don't have any statistical evidence but my first impression of the people in IIT—students and faculty both—was that the per capita incidence of quirky behaviour was significantly higher compared to any other similar-sized group of people I had come across.

Perhaps academic excellence and behavioural quirks are two sides of the same coin. Therefore, the concentration of such people should be expected to be higher in a place like IIT. Or perhaps the environment is such that it fosters and reinforces latent quirky traits which in other more "normal" sets of environment would have remained dormant. Or, perhaps a bit of both is true.

Why would otherwise there be such abundance of anecdotes about idiosyncratic scientists and absent-minded professors which we all have heard and laughed at? Usually, this virus of foolhardiness is latent in the generally straight-laced environment closely supervised by parents and teachers that we all grow up in. Once that supervision gets relaxed with nothing else to replace it in a place like the IIT campus, the contagion spreads faster than a wildfire on a dry prairie.

Wearing slippers—one with a blue strap and the other with red—used to be a proud fashion statement and if someone was found washing his jeans because it was splattered with a few specks of mud, he would be considered a bourgeois prude!

It wasn't the students alone who would be found indulging in such eccentricities, our professors too contributed to the rich repository of entertaining campus tales. There was this professor of mine who would often come on his bicycle to class, wearing a superbly tailored expensive suit with a sparkling white shirt, stiff collar and matching tie but would refuse to wear shoes. His feet pedaling the bicycle would be adorned with old leather slippers.

As a result of all this, if someone was found looking fresh from a recent bath and smooth shave, smelling of cologne, wearing freshly ironed clothes and polished shoes with a smart bag for his notebooks, he would be looked upon with pity as someone who had either lost his mind or someone expecting the impending disaster of a parental visit to the hostel.

CHAPTER SIX

In the Ivory Tower

Friday, 1st August 1980.

While straightening my shirt and combing my hair in front of the mirror early in the morning, I remembered all the First Augusts during my Parle Tilak Vidyalaya years. This used to be the day to participate in an essay or elocution competition on the life and deeds of Lokamanya Tilak in my school on the occasion of his death anniversary. But today I wasn't going to give a speech or present an essay in any competition. This was the first day of my entry into the professional life at TIFR.

"I almost didn't recognize you, all dressed up like a gentleman for a change," my mother said with a smile while handing over lunch box to me. I looked in the mirror and I too almost did not recognize the domesticated, civilized appearance in neatly pressed clothes, polished black formal shoes, freshly shaved chin and a lunch box in hand. So unlike the appearance of the past seven years of IIT—unkempt hair which may have been combed three days ago, a crumpled T-shirt, jeans which were probably blue some years ago, Kolhapuri chappals with a broken strap and a shapeless cloth shoulder bag!

Even while appearing for a job interview during campus placement I don't think I had taken so much trouble for appearance and clothes. I distinctly remember going for even the TIFR interview in an old T-shirt with the IIT Logo and "Hostel 4" printed in large letters on it.

But hey! Today was a new beginning and warranted a bit of celebration, I thought.

When I stepped out of the house my dad said, "Come on I will walk with you to Vileparle station."

And I discovered why, soon enough.

He had a question which had been puzzling him. He (and I suspect a large number of people around me) knew what an electrical engineer or a civil engineer does for a living. But to him, I had given up electrical engineering and had opted for some new-fangled area called "computer science". It wasn't even named as any kind of engineering!

"What exactly is the nature of your job going to be? And what are the future prospects?" he asked.

As if I knew!

Luckily it started drizzling just then and I excused myself saying, "I need to run and reach the station before it starts raining." I sprinted towards the station and caught my train but his question had got me thinking.

I was on my way to start working for TIFR, an organization which had created the first computer in Asia way back in 1956 (which was christened as TIFRAC and dedicated to the nation in 1960 by the then Prime Minister Jawaharlal Nehru). Yet ironically almost two decades later in all of India there were probably not more than a couple of thousand computers actually deployed (and none of them was made in India).

Even a majority of well-educated people like my father had never seen a computer; had no idea what they did or whether they were good for anything and if someone like me could make a career out of working with them.

I remember a heated debate with two of my uncles around this time. On learning that I had opted to do M.Tech. in computer science, their faces acquired a sombre look. I could almost read their expression: "Eh! You are wasting your time!" One of them, who used to work in a famous cigarette company, actually said, "It is just a new fad. My company installed a new computer in our accounts section recently by spending a few million rupees! "It can do nothing more than what I have been doing all these years for a fraction of that cost. It is so dumb that even if a single purchase order contains a small mistake, like a misspelt supplier name, it throws out the whole batch."

"Absolutely right," said the other uncle, who used to work in a government department. "It is the same story in my office too."

"If the computers start doing whatever we have been doing so well for years, what then are we suppose to do? Stay at home? Only when this creates legions of unemployed workers in the country, will the government wake up to this menace."

The cigarette company uncle was parroting the argument he must have heard in some union meeting. My dad was getting restless, probably because of the fear that I was going to get lynched in the future for contributing to this catastrophe.

Their argument—"What can this silly machine do which I can't do at a fraction of the cost"—was in a sense the same as Shakuntala Devi's claim that she could do calculations faster than any computer.

This argument was wrong on three counts.

First of all, that "silly" machine wasn't meant to "replace" what they were "capable" of doing. Rather it was meant to do all the tasks which they need not have done, all the tasks for which their human intelligence wasn't required. It was meant to free them up to do more of what their intelligent minds were really capable of.

Second, while at the present size and scale of their companies they could have managed adequately without the computers, as their respective companies grew, they weren't going to be able to cope up with the increased workload at larger scale and faster rate of growth.

The third was a more subtle issue. The political-economic environment of those days had ensured that

Indian companies had no fear of competition from high quality, efficient, international companies engaged in the same business as theirs. Therefore, they had no need, incentive or drive to modernize or to become efficient using technology such as computers. As time was to teach us, the state of affairs caused by the business environment of state-protected monopolies wasn't going to last forever. When that protection ended—as it did a few years later—those who weren't prepared for the competition weren't going to last.

While this may have been recognized by the captains of the industry then, it was far from apparent to ordinary people like us.

However, I could not say any of these things to my uncles at that time.

While I was sure I was right, I hadn't really "seen" the wonderful world of computers till then myself. I was hoping TIFR would provide that opportunity because outside of a few organizations like TIFR, the landscape was more or less only a few steps beyond the stone age of computing.

Generally, at that time the political environment in our country was dominated by socialistic thinking—*big business*, *technology*, *automation* were evil words. Computers were deemed at worst the villains responsible for stealing the daily bread from hard working people and at best a new-fangled capitalist idea with no real ability to impact ordinary society for the better!

The race between a horse-drawn carriage and a bus in the movie *Naya Daur* (although the movie was made in 1957) still symbolized common perception of the place of technology in our lives.

How wrong history was going to prove us in the next three decades!

Getting acclimatized to TIFR was no problem at all. The environment and culture was much the same as in

IIT. I quickly realized on the first day itself that I need not have spent so much time in front of the mirror to look respectable on the first day of my job! I could have gone to work in much the same attire as I was used to on IIT campus and still would have fitted in quite nicely!

There were no classes, lectures and examination in TIFR, nevertheless it was in spirit an educational institute. Academic excellence was all that mattered there and productivity was measured by the number of research papers one published. Dr Homi Bhabha's grand vision supported by funding from the House of Tatas had helped establish TIFR in 1945. With world-class infrastructure and facilities for fundamental research in physics and mathematics (and other allied fields like molecular biology), TIFR had attracted eminent scientists, such as Prof. Jayant Naralikar, from all over India.

I am not sure whether computer science as an independent branch of research was at the top of the agenda at TIFR. However, there were two separate groups—NSCDCT (National Centre for Software Development and Computing Technology) headed by Prof. Narasimhan and SDS (Speech and Digital Systems) headed by Prof. P.V.S. Rao, which were actively engaged in interesting developments in computer science. I had heard Prof. Narasimhan's lectures in IIT and had interacted with Prof. Ramani, who was my examiner for M.Tech. thesis.

Then there was Dr Cooper, who had interviewed me for the job at TIFR.

I started working as a scientific officer in Dr Cooper's group. At that time we were engaged in a project for the Department of Defence. We were chartered to develop a new kind of radar with highly intelligent software for tracking aircraft using the radar for the Indian Air Force.

There were about twenty of us engineers from various premier engineering institutes like IITs and BITS in the team, rubbing shoulders with a bunch of Air Force officers who were also part of the team. The domain expertise of the officers and the technology know-how of engineers were expected to be married to create the new system.

I was, of course, the baby of the team; everybody else had been working on this project for a long time. As a result of this, and also because of the more or less laissez-faire culture of TIFR, I had ample opportunity to observe the atmosphere in my group as well as the larger environment of TIFR.

The first (not-so-pleasant) realization was—as I mentioned earlier—that computer science wasn't at the top of the research agenda for TIFR. The prevalent view seemed be that physics and mathematics were the only two areas which qualified as "pure sciences" and research in those areas was the only research that was qualified as "fundamental".

If you have watched the American TV serial *Big Bang Theory*, the point of view expressed by the character of Sheldon Cooper in it captures the exact sentiment one went through at TIFR in those days.

Computer science was deemed a sub-discipline in "applied" mathematics with the qualifier "applied" considered a bad word. This view that segregated different branches of scientific inquiry into categories of 'more important' and 'less important' was beyond my understanding. In any case, I was the smallest cog in a big wheel and it did not affect my enjoyment of the work I was engaged in.

Apart from this fundamental ideological surprise, the rest of the environment in TIFR was fabulous. Unlike a business or professional organization, there were no set, rigid rules, processes or policies which dictated what you could or could not do. There was no straightjacketing, no defined set of activities, and no externally defined course for you to follow.

You scoped out the nature of your work. You decided where you fitted in the team you were working with. You also decided what course you were going to take and how you were going to address the technical or scientific problem that you yourself had identified. If you felt like it, you could change your current plan and pursue a different direction to solve your problems.

Of course, at the end of the day, the output mattered, the quality of solutions you created mattered, how quickly you got there mattered but all of that was not pre-specified and imposed on you by somebody else.

While engaged in the mainstream work which you were responsible for, you had the freedom to engage in any other activities or projects which took your fancy in your spare time. And, if you did produce something worthwhile through these voluntary efforts, you were applauded just as loudly.

TIFR was often a meeting place for eminent scientists and researchers from all over the world. When they visited they would hold seminars and lectures about their ongoing work. That provided an excellent opportunity to learn about the latest developments even in fields which had nothing to do with your own area of specialization. I probably understood a fraction of what was being talked in such meetings but the inspirational value of listening to eminent visiting academicians was immense.

The last, but for me the most important, institution within TIFR was its library. I fell head-over-heels in love with this library the very first time I visited it. Books containing the works of famous scientists from classical times to the current era (I read Charles Darwin's *The Voyage of the Beagle* here), periodicals devoted to science and technology from all over the world and textbooks on any scientific and technological subject under the sun could be found here.

IIT also had a large and respectable library. However, it was a place where you went only when you had to. The staff in the IIT library for some unknown reason considered chasing students out as soon as possible as one of their duties. In TIFR you could go to the library at any time of the day or night, pick up a book and read anything for any length of time.

This library was my refuge for the first three months after I joined TIFR. Sometimes an adversity turns out to be a boon. For the first three months, I had no assigned place to sit and work. I would occupy any vacant table in the room where our team was working but would be forced to shift place when the rightful occupant returned from his tea break or visit to the laboratory. Tired of this game of musical chairs I decided to shift my base to the library.

I would sit there and do some of my work, take a break and pick up a journal with the latest papers on computational complexity theory or programming language semantics—subjects not related to my assigned task but for which I had a fascination. Then I would spend a few hours learning about new, exciting developments in computer science, go back to my work, take another break and pick up a popular science magazine with articles on esoteric scientific developments written for lay people like me and so on. This was for me like a seven-course dinner where every course was a dessert.

Finally I was given my own table in Dr Cooper's team room.

Until then the only kind of computers I had played with were the ancient dinosaurs—Minsk II and EC-1030 in IIT. The only way you could interact with them was through a paper tape or a deck of punched cards. You couldn't know how highly the computer thought of what you considered a great piece of software until the next day when the computer disdainfully spat your card deck out with a printout of errors. You worked like the proverbial lizard trying to climb the wall: three steps forward, two steps back.

In TIFR I had my first encounter with a truly modern, interactive computing environment with a terminal right next to my desk, which was connected to a powerful mainframe called DEC-10 housed in the deep bowels of the TIFR building.

I could type in my program directly on the keyboard and find out what was working and what wasn't instantaneously!

Most of you today cannot identify with the exhilaration of this freedom from the clutches of card-punching machine or the euphoria of being able to directly interact with a computer.

Developing a program which used to be a matter of weeks became an affair of a few hours! Of course, things like networked computers or Internet were still a decade or so in the future. Here each computer was an island. There was no e-mail, no Google, no Wi-Fi, no social media. But still the computing facilities available to me were then among the best in the world.

As I mentioned earlier, this was a project being executed for the Indian Air Force and a bunch of IAF officers were working as part of the team. They had two-fold function. Provide their domain knowledge as a user of the radar system, which we were developing and also learn the technical details of the system that was being designed. So that after the prototype was built and successfully tested they could take over its deployment and subsequent maintenance.

Working with people who had been conditioned in the rigid traditions of defence forces was a bit of a clash of cultures which lead to many amusing incidents.

For instance, one day I found that someone had taken the pain of putting a bold stamp on each page of a nearly 400-page TTL data book, saying, "Top Secret".

A TTL data book is a technical book published by manufacturers of the semiconductor integrated circuit chips that gives detailed technical information about each chip. This information is required when you are designing a circuit using these chips as components. Many of the chips mentioned in that book were being used by us in the system that was being designed by our team.

Someone had decided that since the project was a sensitive defence project and details of the design of the system were confidential, all documentation related to the project was classified material. As a principle, of course, this was warranted. However, the funny thing was that, that particular data book was a freely available commodity which anyone could buy for a few rupees from Lamington Road in Mumbai!

Of course, this blind adherence to rules and procedures wasn't the sole preserve of our team. After all TIFR too was a government organization. And despite all the "out-of-the-box thinking" and "break-the-mould" culture that was cultivated by the researchers, the administrative machinery in TIFR was as bureaucratic and hidebound in blindly following the letter of the rule rather than the spirit as any other government organization.

My experience in IIT was no different; the conflict with the academic office while doing M.Tech. was still fresh in my mind.

A simple matter of carrying shuttlecocks and rackets to play badminton after work through the gate security in and out of the TIFR campus also used to turn into a struggle (even when both shuttles and rackets were bought by us). When convincing the security personnel that this was, in fact, not scientific equipment which we were trying to smuggle in or out of the campus proved futile, we had to go all the way to the head of the administration to get a written permission to do so!

Fortunately, during the course of a usual day, I had little need or occasion to tangle with this side of the institute. And when some such inane argument did trigger a headache, going to the West Canteen and cooling off over a hot cup of tea—while gazing over the scenic garden and tranquil sea from the window—was an effective remedy. In fact, the canteen and the fabulous fare it provided was an important factor in making my stint in TIFR a pleasure.

By the time I started working in TIFR on the real project which Dr Cooper's group was engaged in, most of the core development had already got over and the project was in the last stages of completion. My involvement in it was rather peripheral.

However, just about that time the two groups in TIFR devoted to R&D in computer science and technology, called NCSDCT and SDS (despite sometime being rivals of each other) had initiated a joint effort related to local area networking and parallel computing, which I got assigned to.

Interconnecting computers using high-speed communication technologies like ethernets was a recent development then. While the technology to make computers talk to each other and exchange information was fully developed in research labs like Xerox PARC, its commercial usage was still nascent. And the kind of innovative things one could do to fully exploit the potential of a network of computers was still being explored.

This was an exciting field, and one of the important areas on which our project was focused on was parallel computing where a group of networked computers act collaboratively to solve complex computing problems, which would otherwise take any single computer a very long time to solve.

However, in order to make that happen, a great deal of basic software programs have to be developed; like an operating system that can coordinate the activities of the members of a group of networked computers, an appropriate programming language to write programs to perform computations in parallel on multiple individual computers in the network, a tool called a compiler that can translate this programming language into a form that the computers can understand, a system to manage the data/information that these programs need to use by distributing it across the group of networked computers, etc.

The team had already designed such a "parallel computing" programming language called CCN-Pascal and I was assigned to develop the compiler for this programming language. This was exciting work and in a sense a progression from where I had left my M.Tech. project in IIT which was also focused on developing some new optimizing techniques for compilers.

The new challenge here was that this was a compiler for a parallel computing programming language. The work progressed rapidly and pretty soon I got the opportunity to work on the distributed data management system as well involving new challenges to address efficient distribution of data across the network, design of efficient methods for quick retrieval of the stored data that may be located at one computer in the network but required at another and so on.

While this was going on I was told to start writing research papers and get them published as soon as possible. However, I wasn't sure this was the right time to start spending time on writing papers. I hadn't really completed all the development.

At best what was completed was a partially working laboratory prototype. There were loose ends, weak areas and kinks which needed to be ironed out. And, the software that was developed wasn't really tried out in the real world! The rubber had yet to meet the road and there was considerable effort that was required before one could do so.

However, these were not the questions that seemed to be troubling anyone around. Getting a paper published was the pinnacle of achievement in a setting like TIFR. Getting it done before anybody else established your primacy. And that seemed to matter more even if the development was not quite complete and the outcomes not yet really useful.

This ivory-tower thinking was proving to be a little difficult for me. In any case my employment contract with TIFR was for three years and that period was coming to an end. So I never bothered to discuss the issue of publishing papers or why I wasn't keen on doing it then with anyone (as it happened some of that work did get published after I left TIFR. One of my colleagues and a close friend Dr Sanyal felt it was a waste to let it languish in the archives of TIFR and took the trouble to write it and publish it).

The three years spent in TIFR were exciting. We were working at the leading edge of the rapidly developing computing technology, trying to solve unsolved problems in areas such as parallel computing and distributed databases. All around me, my other colleagues were equally immersed in developing unheard of applications of computer science; understanding and reproducing human speech, tracking airplanes using a radar, creating computing equipment rugged enough to be used in a truck moving in a sandstorm where temperatures soared above 50-degree Celsius.

There were others pushing the limits of the science itself, exploring new questions: what is the "meaning" of a computer program? How can one prove a program "correct" so that it may never need to be tested? How to determine what is the most efficient method to solve a complex problem? And so on.

The environment in TIFR was conducive to dream such seemingly impossible dreams and work to make them a reality. And yet I started feeling that there was a chasm between the real world and the world we were inhabiting in TIFR.

Perhaps that was by design. Perhaps it was a deliberate strategy to focus on developing the science that can solve the problems of tomorrow and not worry about applying existing technology to solve the problems of today.

I was too lowly a cog in the machine to be privy to such long-term vision. And, on second thoughts, perhaps it was appropriate that somebody was focusing on tomorrow rather than today.

However, that wasn't my cup of tea. To be sure my own group led by Dr Cooper had its feet firmly grounded in the present, but he seemed a rarity in TIFR. Also, I was vaguely aware that he and his key lieutenants were making their own plans to plunge into the real world outside.

I had also already made up my mind that I would rather spend the next few years of my career in a more "industrial" environment where whatever I did was going to be actually used by someone.

TIFR was a big buyer of the latest and greatest computing and related technology that was on offer and as result there was ongoing interaction with people representing several technology companies keen on selling their equipment to TIFR.

These interactions had made me aware of a new, vibrant and dynamic field that was sprouting in the commercial world outside the ivory tower of the academia which I had been a part of for ten years, from 1973 to 1983.

Besides the opportunities to be a contributor to this growing industry, the potential financial rewards appeared undoubtedly more interesting than the academic life.

The next step for me therefore was going and joining a small company called Patni Computer Systems.

CHAPTER SEVEN

From Utopia to Reality

There were mixed feelings, as I made my way into the industry outside the academic utopia and joined a small company called Patni Computer Systems. There was trepidation because I was completely unaware of what was going on in the business world. My environment until then was driven by things that were intellectually intriguing and not by those that made money; proving a theorem was more important than making a profit. Producing a mathematical proof of correctness of a computer program was valued more than making that program actually run successfully on a computer.

I wasn't sure to what extent my ten years' learning was going to be useful in making a successful career in this new environment. There was also the double whammy of juggling a new job and the new role of a husband because I had recently got married to Anju. That was an entirely new equation and all my knowledge of discrete mathematics wasn't going to help solve it. To keep the household happy one needs to develop different skills.

Patni Computer Systems was a small company started by three brothers—Gajendra, Naren and Ashok. Ashok was from IIT Mumbai. While I didn't know him when he was in IIT, I had heard about him through others on the campus who knew him. That was one of the factors in deciding to join a then small and unknown company.

More importantly, two of my close friends from IIT, Arvind Kher and Vijay Khare, were working there. Whatever I had heard from them convinced me that culturally I wouldn't feel like an alien there. Moreover at that time it seemed more prudent to hope to grow to be a big fish starting in a small pond than running the risk of forever remaining a small fish in a big pond.

About a hundred people spread between an office in Raheja Chambers at Nariman Point and a small factory in Saki Naka in Mumbai was the entire extent of the company then.

"An IT company had a *factory,*" one would wonder! That isn't the general view of an IT company today.

The general picture of an IT company is that of a battery of programmers hammering away at their keyboards and developing or maintaining software programs for customers in every corner of the world.

When I joined Patni Computer Systems in 1983, IT business, by and large, was a "manufacturing" business. Except Tata Consultancy Services (TCS), almost every other IT company was primarily focused on manufacturing and selling computers to other businesses in India.

Of course, one may quite justifiably laugh now at the activities in these factories being defined as "manufacturing". From an engineering point of view, these activities were no more than building a house using Lego bricks.

No Indian company then (with rare and notable exceptions like ORG—a company that nobody remembers now and that did not last long) was investing in designing their own computers or computing technology. Every other company—be it Patni, HCL, Wipro, ICIM (ICL) or Hinditron—had licensed technology from some American or European computer manufacturer. Under this license, they would import ready-to-assemble kits (or even completely built units) of computers from their principles—often yesterday's models made by these principles.

Manufacturing, therefore, mostly consisted of screwing together these parts following instructions which were only a little more complicated than "insert part A into slot B" and hey presto, a shining new computer was ready to be installed! Software development, if at all, was an indulgence to be engaged in only if it helped sell the computers being so manufactured. The "factory" therefore was the centre of attention.

This was a far cry from the heady achievements of organizations like TIFR that had built TIFRAC—one of the earliest computers in Asia, fully designed and developed in India a couple of decades earlier.

TIFR or the political leadership or the industry captains of that time clearly never saw the potential and did not see the need to commercialize the technology developed via TIFRAC.

Perhaps computing technology was considered an unaffordable luxury for a poor nation struggling to meet the basic needs of it populace. The common adage of the time seemed to be, "If something can be done by a person why do you pay for a machine to do so".

This was to be proved a fallacious argument later.

Time was to prove that computers don't have to be viewed as villains that leave hard working people destitute. On the contrary, computers can be a powerful tool to make the same hard working people more productive. Computers can actually create more opportunities for people rather than usurping them and last but not the least, this tool can actually help address those very social problems, which were accorded higher priority compared to modernizing technology, in a multitude of different ways.

However, hindsight is always 20-20. The tide was to turn only after several decades.

At that time leading computer companies like IBM had been banished from India and barriers had been erected in acquiring advanced technology from outside in a fit of socialistic backlash.

Businesses at large too had little incentive in adopting modern technology in those days. Businesses are driven by profits. Profits are affected by competition. Competition drives productivity and innovation. And technology provides the catalyst for both increasing productivity and innovation.

In an environment that created state-sanctioned monopolies, which gave them protected markets, eliminated the freedom of choice from consumers, there was no incentive for businesses to employ modern technology to either increase productivity or to create innovative products.

This of course is an overly simplistic picture but nevertheless not too far from truth.

There was another factor contributing to the dearth of computing technology in India then. The developed world viewed India with suspicion because of our political closeness to the USSR. Even if a business managed to overcome the internal barriers to importing modern technology, the developed world wouldn't easily let it be exported to India from their factories, fearing it would be passed on to the rival super power.

This was then the situation I found myself in, when I dipped my toe into this new world of Indian information-technology industry in the early nineteen eighties.

It appeared to me quickly enough that my career was not going to be defined by my ability to create new cutting-edge computers or software. It was going to depend on finding new ways to convince a potential customer to adopt existing computing technology that was often on the verge of being superseded by something new in the rest of the world.

Or so I thought then. That was to change rapidly too due to a completely different chain of events.

After I started working for Patni as a senior software engineer, I began to gradually understand our customers, their circumstances and needs.

In very broad terms they fell into two categories. There were big-name, well-established business houses. All of these were already using computers as an integral part of their operations. These enterprises were usually looking to replace their superannuated computing platforms by more modern technology. Most of them had installed systems sold to them by companies like IBM, which had been ousted from India a few years earlier and the companies had therefore stayed stuck without a viable upgrade path.

The other category consisted of those who had spent little or nothing on computerization and were probably trying to figure out how this new-fangled technology would fit into their businesses and help them grow.

I had spent my formative years in a place like TIFR where most modern technology that the world had to offer was easily accessible. Therefore, in the beginning many of the conversations with customers from both categories were very "educational" to say the least.

There was this cement company that had decided to purchase a new computer from Patni. They were already using for some years an old relic sold to them by IBM called IBM 1401.

The first surprise to me was that IBM 1401 was still alive and kicking and the company was actively using it for their back office—payroll, accounting etc. The first 1401 was sold commercially by IBM in 1959—almost 25 years earlier. Outside India probably the only place it could be found was in museums.

And here it was the main computing workhorse of a major big-name company in India!

I suppressed the surprise on my face with some efforts and spent some time extolling the virtues of the computer system we were trying to sell them. During the conversation I asked "So how are you planning to employ this wonderful new machine?"

I was in for another surprise.

"The first thing you must prove to us is that your computer can run all our 1401 programs AS-THEY-STAND without needing to make any change what-so-ever," I was told.

"Huh! If all you want to do is to make this new computer behave exactly as your ageing 1401, why do you want to spend so much money to buy a new computer?" was my naïve reaction—in my own mind, of course. I didn't dare say this publicly.

As I learnt later my reaction was uncalled for. But I had no knowledge then of the compulsions and constraints under which a running business must operate. Purely simulating a 1401 on a much more modern and powerful computer wasn't the only thing they were planning to do. But they had to keep their bread-and-butter processes critical to their business running uninterrupted while they were modernizing in parallel.

So the first task I had to accomplish was to simulate a 1401 on our new computer and validate that all their 1401 programs will run without any change.

The irony was that I had just spent three years studying and contributing to cutting-edge technologies like parallel computing and relational databases (which was still a technology under active academic research then and hadn't yet appeared in any commercial products), and here I was trying to unravel the mysteries of a two-and-a-half-decade-old, obsolete computer. But this was reality. This was the need of the market our company was in.

The first impression was that the market seemed to lack the vision, the desire and the large upfront capital required to use the power of computing to truly innovate and create path-breaking products and business processes.

This was again an incorrect and unfair assessment. Conditioned as I was in a freewheeling academic environment, there was a lot to learn about the real world.

The need for large capital investments was real; for example, the amount of computing power you can purchase today for fifteen or twenty thousand rupees in the form of a smartphone or a tablet would have required forty or fifty lakh rupees then.

At a time when the valuations of the best-performing companies were at best in hundreds of crores of rupees and not hundreds of thousands of crores as they are now, spending fifty lakh on a device with unproven potential wasn't an easy decision to make even for the richest of companies.

Then there were potential buyers with a very different take on computerization. For many of them buying a computer was an adventurous decision. Many a time, it wasn't quite clear how exactly this technology could be used to make a difference to their business. They were used to spending large sums of money on tangible goods which could be touched, felt and weighed but ... software?

How do you value something you couldn't measure in terms of neat quantifiable parameters? How do you put a price tag on something the impact of which on the business couldn't be immediately measured?

They were finding it hard to answer these kinds of questions.

We also were finding it difficult to justify the value of software because, first, we ourselves weren't quite sure about how to demonstrate a causal relationship between a software application and tangible business values like revenue and profits.

Second, even when we could show some such relationship, understanding the nature of that relationship required some minimum level of appreciation of computing technology that many of these potential buyers seemed to lack.

The net result used to be a demand for even the most complex software systems to be provided for free in return for agreeing to buy the computer for a price we were asking.

The usual conversation in essence in these situations used to be—

"All right! I will agree to pay you so and so amount for your computer. Because I can show this shining new machine with mysteriously blinking lights to everyone and my CFO and nobody will question my decision to spend so much of money. However what can I show in return if I pay you for your software?"

This was not too different from a "buy three soaps and I will give you a tooth paste for free" type of offers that they were used to dealing with.

There was, of course, a simple remedy to this situation. Bury the price of the software supposedly being given free somewhere in the price list of the computer hardware which was being sold. That is what most of the companies in a business similar to ours wound up doing. It took a long time and enough computer literacy to build up, for these purchasers (and also to sellers like us) to appreciate the value of software.

The kind of confusion that existed while determining the price of software wasn't entirely absent in determining the price of a computer either.

Suppose that two companies are offering to sell you their respective computers at different prices. Then how do you decide whether the "higher" price being asked for by company A as compared to company B is worth paying because their computer is more "powerful" than company B's? How do you determine the "power" of these computers (whatever that might mean)?

The question created a strange demand from the potential buyers that we had to put up with. Now when I look back, it seems very funny but at that time it was a big headache and the cause of many sleepless nights spent in the office. This was something called *benchmark*.

A benchmark in common parlance is a widely accepted standard for something against which other similar things can be measured and compared. For example, the benchmark for the unit of measure of "length" used to be a bar of platinum-iridium alloy kept at the International Bureau of Weights and Measures in Paris. Any ruler could be compared with the length of this bar to determine how accurately that ruler could measure lengths. This benchmark was of course changed later and the modern definition of the benchmark for a "meter" is in terms of the number of wave lengths of light of a particular frequency.

There was no such benchmark defined and accepted by a wide enough audience to determine the "power" of a computer.

Still our customers would demand that we "prove" to them that our computer was more powerful than some other company's computers. How do we do that? We couldn't ask the customer to define what they meant by "more powerful". It was obvious that they couldn't answer this question either.

To be sure, there were internationally published benchmarks for computers—like Dhrystone or Linpac. However, all of them were designed to measure only some specific characteristic of a computer under controlled conditions.

In real-life usage, neither would those exact controlled conditions be found nor could the relevance of the specific attribute being measured be ascertained. Therefore, the value of these standard benchmarks in real-life usage was extremely dubious.

Nevertheless, everybody wanted the "fastest" computer that money could buy. This was like buying a Hennessey Venom GT car that runs at 450 kilometers per hour and costs a million dollars or more to drive on Mumbai roads *only* because you want to cut down your driving time from Andheri to Nariman Point to ten minutes!

Some of the customers were more pragmatic. They would put together a random collection of computer programs that were supposedly representative of the kind of work they were planning to do eventually on the computer if they purchased it.

We were required to show that this suite of programs runs faster on our computer than some other computers which they were considering. In principle, this was a fine strategy. In reality, designing such benchmarks that can simulate the eventual real usage of the computer with sufficient fidelity is a fiendishly difficult endeavour.

It was rare to find a potential buyer or even the "expert" consultant whom they sometimes engaged to help them, with the ability or the knowledge to do so. Most often this "benchmark" suite would be a motley collection of programs hurriedly put together for no discernible reason. It would have been futile to argue or to try to educate them about this. Any arguments would have been construed as an admission that our computer wasn't good enough for their purpose!

So we would meekly accept their "benchmarks" and a monumental drama would begin, to get them running and running as fast as we could make them on our systems.

First of all, we had to locate a computer with exactly identical configuration as that which we had offered to our customer. The performance of a computer depends on a myriad of factors (one reason why any "standard" benchmark is usually quite useless to prove "satisfactory" performance). Unless each of these factors in the computer used for running the benchmark matches exactly with the offered computer (which hasn't been fully built yet) the results of the benchmark are quite meaningless.

In those days, computers were not being mass produced and stocked in anticipation of future sales. Each computer was built only after a confirmed order was received from a customer. As a result usually we wouldn't have an exactly matching computer in our labs or factory available to run the benchmark.

So the hunt would begin. Had we sold a computer with matching configuration to some other customer in the past? Would they agree to let us use it for running this benchmark? Could we patch together the required configuration quickly by temporarily adding borrowed modules and devices (such as additional memory boards or disk drives)?

Usually the only time an existing customer would allow us to use their installed system used to be in the middle of the night. We beggars could not be choosers. So when everybody else would be deep in dreamland we would be toiling fuelled by large doses of caffeine.

The bright side of all this was—

We always knew that given the naïve design of most of these benchmarks we would be able to apply our knowledge and some creativity to produce any answer that the customer wanted to see while remaining completely honest and ethical!

The funny thing was everybody else—all our competitors—would also be doing to same thing. In the end, after having made all the competing vendors like us run these benchmarks, whether the customer was in a position to make a better informed decision was very questionable.

But hey! We had no complaints. We were, in fact, more than happy if we could sell our computers, even though it had cost us a few sleepless nights. And I guess the customers too were happy to have got their Hennessey Venom GT because of their benchmarks!

Determining whether the computer system you are about to buy has the capacity to handle the tasks that you want it to perform remains to this day more of an art than science.

What has changed is the fall in prices of computing power. You can now very easily afford to play safe and over-provide computing horse-power for very little extra money. However, at a time and place when a computer less powerful than your current smart phone's processor cost 500 times more than the price of that phone, the question whether it can sort a file containing 1,00,000 data records in 160 seconds or 148 seconds, was a major factor influencing the decision to buy it or not buy it.

Often we would get entangled in issues that had nothing to do with technology.

There was this fertilizer company to whom we had sold a large computer system. Everything was ready in our factory, including several large software applications we had built for them. We were only waiting for the site of their computer centre to be ready.

And we got an urgent call for an emergency meeting. In the meeting we were told—"There is some trouble with the worker's union. We have heard that plans are being made to hold demonstrations against computerization and it is possible that company gates may be blocked to prevent us from bringing the computer in."

We were surprised. While we had nothing to do with their problems, we had heard from some of them in the past that this whole plan of computerization was explained to the workers and their union officials and an agreement to go ahead been obtained. What had changed since then we had no clue, however the problem had to be solved.

So once again we realized we had to sacrifice a good night's sleep. We had to deliver the computer and all associated equipment in the dead of the night and work overnight to completely install everything and get everything alive and kicking before the dawn broke.

Everything went according to the plan. Before anybody else in the factory had woken up and brushed their teeth, we were on our way home in a taxi.

Things, of course, weren't quite hunky-dory as we had imagined while driving home half asleep. Apparently there were demonstrations in front of the computer centre the next day and the battle with the workers simmered for quite some time before it got resolved and all the fancy technology and software we had installed started being used productively.

Not all such challenges had a happy ending though.

We were negotiating with a defence laboratory in Bangalore for supply of the most advanced computer in our product line that they wanted to use for some cutting-edge research in semiconductor chip design.

In the first two meetings itself it was apparent that this was a refreshingly different customer compared to all the others whom I had come in contact with until then. They were experts in their own field and very knowledgeable about the technology that they wanted from us.

Discussions with them used to keep us on our toes. Understanding their problem, suggesting solutions to address it used to be extremely challenging and educational for us. We were looking forward to actually getting down to putting together the solution but that required importing some, then cutting-edge, technology from America and that is where the obstacles arose.

Those were the days of Cold War. Perhaps India was being viewed as leaning towards the Soviet camp. As a result, export of high technology to India may have been looked upon with a great deal of suspicion. Perhaps it was felt that India might use it for weapon's research or might make this technology available to the "other side"! Whatever the reasons may be, we were unable to secure the license to import the required technology from the US and the whole project got cancelled.

The funny thing is—a few years later we were designing a comprehensive solution to automate the operations of a large steel plant in India that required exactly the same technology. This time there were no barriers at all in acquiring it. And that wasn't all. Along with the systems a whole bunch of American experts too came and spent a couple of years in India to work together with us to develop the software!

A lot of water had flown under the political bridge in the intervening few years.

In the nineteen eighties, it was not as if only small companies like us were at the receiving end of this US policy of controlling the availability of technology to Indian enterprises. Even the Government of India was denied permission to import the Cray supercomputer that the government wanted to buy for weather research.

Perhaps as a reaction to that, the Centre for Development of Advanced Computing (CDAC) was formed. CDAC under the leadership of Dr Vijay Bhatkar created the completely indigenous Param supercomputer within two years.

It was perhaps the first significant and totally indigenous development in the field of computing since TIFRAC. Param attracted a great deal of worldwide attention during the Zurich Supercomputing show in 1990 due to its innovative design and stellar performance.

I must narrate one more incidence that is truly an eye opener.

For the first time it made me realize that there sometimes is a sinister side to even the most exciting technological developments. That the greatest feats of intellectual achievements could sometimes be swords that make wounds, depending on the hands that wield them.

We were in discussions with a company with a well-known brand then. They were considering purchasing a large computer system including a large suite of software applications as a part of a major modernization programme.

We had had several discussions and presentations about the capabilities of our computers. We had spent time understanding their business requirements so that we could propose the right software to be developed to meet those requirements.

We had spent a few long days and nights to carefully prepare our presentation and to ensure we had correctly addressed all their business requirements.

The day dawned when we had to make a final presentation to their top management and describe the complete solution that we had thought of.

The presentation began and suddenly one of their top officials—a member of their board of directors stopped me. "All this technical mumbo-jumbo you can discuss with my EDP Manager (The term CIO—Chief Information Officer, was unknown then). All I want to know is how your computer can help me reduce my staff strength and what is the number of people I can remove from the company?" he asked.

I was flabbergasted.

Was the computer a replacement for people?

I had seen and participated in computers being used in innovative applications such as tracking enemy airplanes using radars or understanding speech or monitoring the ECG of a heart patient. All of these applications represented tasks generally carried out by people. None of them however were meant to replace the people but to make them more productive, reduce their fatigue, make them less error prone, enable them to do things they couldn't do unaided.

I wasn't sure I had heard the question correctly.

So I asked, "But why do you want to let go your staff?"

"How else can my company afford to buy this computer of yours unless I can reduce my cost of production and increase my profits"?

I tried to answer with a counter question,

But do you think reducing the staff is the best way to reduce your cost of production? We have spent time with your people to understand your processes and have found excellent opportunities to reduce your costs by optimizing your shop-floor scheduling and inventory management. Let me explain to you how the software we propose to develop will help.

He wouldn't even let me complete—

"No, no, no, no, all these are theories. The lowest hanging fruit is reduction in manpower and unless you can show me how your computer will enable us to achieve that I am not sure I want to buy it."

And he just walked out of the meeting.

We didn't know what to say and how to respond. We finished the rest of the presentation in a desultory fashion for the remaining attendees and left. They never bought our computer. Whether they did from some other company, I never found out.

CHAPTER EIGHT

The Dawn of a New Era

The first few years in Patni were a breeze while I was coming to grips with the real world of our customers; the compulsions and constraints under which they operated and in understanding how we could succeed by solving their problems.

Purely engineering problems, however complex, usually have neat mathematical techniques to solve them. There are structured methods to make even seemingly intractable problems involving a large number of variables tractable.

The problems that I had to deal with now revolved around the most unpredictable variable of all—human beings, whose reactions and responses couldn't be captured in neat equations, at least not by the kind which I had been taught in IIT.

Just because I had got a degree from a prestigious institute didn't mean all that I needed to learn had been learned.

By saying that I don't mean to sound as if I agree with facetious expressions such as: "The real learning starts only after you get your degree and get out of your college" or "half of what I learned in school I never used in the real world and the other half I promptly forgot the moment I got out" or something to that effect.

Such flippancy may get a bit of applause from an audience but has little value or a grain of truth in it otherwise. Without exception, everything that I learned in IIT or TIFR I wound up using sometime or the other. But that alone wasn't enough. I couldn't afford to stop learning!

This new college wasn't necessarily as congenial as IIT campus was. There was no guiding hand, no benevolent tutor to answer queries, no reference library to look up readymade solutions. You were responsible for your own success or failure.

At the same time, it was fun to stumble, fall on your face, realize your limitations, learn a new fact of life, brace yourself and bounce back.

We were a young crowd in Patni and for most of us it was a first job. The lack of experience was in a way a blessing. Every adversity was a challenge and being able to successfully address it was its own reward.

Consider the overnights which we pulled off while preparing for the stupid benchmarks our customers wanted run. We would often struggle non-stop from Saturday morning till Sunday night, with only a hurriedly snatched chai and vada-pav from the street to keep us going.

Yet, as we trudged our weary feet home, hardly anyone cursed his luck or called his job modern-day slavery. More often than not one of us would have found some obscure trick, some perfectly legitimate sleight of hand to get the benchmark working. And we marched homeward with elated heart.

This feeling was similar to going on a long monsoon hike to Harishchandra Gadh or Nane Ghat, wading through rain, mud and untamed forests; at the end of the day your bones would creak and muscles scream but your mind would swim in an extra dose of serotonin and dopamine—the happiness hormones!

Life in an IT company wasn't easy. We may have been selling modern technology to our customers but that didn't mean it was available in abundance for our own use.

I had just spent a long, hard weekend getting a crucial set of programs working properly; these were to be shown to a customer on Monday morning. As usual I had gone home, late on Sunday, tired but triumphant.

I reached our Sakinaka factory very early on Monday, around 8 a.m., because I wanted to set up everything and do a dry run before the customer turned up. I was too early. Nobody else had come in yet. The computer on which this demonstration was to happen was standing in a corner of the lab. I switched it on, and nothing happened!

"Huh! What the xxxx!"

I had shut it down the previous night at 10 p.m. and it was working just fine then. The main power supply was certainly on because I myself had just turned on all the air-conditioners and lights. Perhaps a fuse had blown in the switchboard, I thought. So I opened it and found no problem there.

I could feel beads of sweat on my forehead in the near-freezing temperature of the lab. Computers in those days had rows of blinking lights on the front panel. Usually one did not pay attention to them because they changed so rapidly and in such complicated combinations that just looking at them could tell you nothing at all about what was happening inside the computer.

Yet somewhere at the back of my mind these patterns, which I had "seen" countless times but never "observed", were recorded over a period of time. As I stood before the dead computer with shaky legs and sweaty palms wondering what to do, I realized that while the master terminal of the computer was stubbornly displaying a jet-black screen, some of these front-panel lights were twinkling. I developed a nagging feeling that the blinking wasn't "normal".

Like a drowning man clutching at last straw, I thought of opening the front panel to take a peep inside. Strictly speaking, I wasn't quite authorized to do so. But I thought, "What the heck, the day is a disaster anyway if this computer does not start up, how much worse can it get?"

So I opened the front panel and there it was—the computer was laughing at me through a gaping hole where two memory boards should have been! Somebody had removed them between 10 p.m. and 8 a.m.

There was no time to investigate the mystery of the missing memory boards; no time to follow the protocol—of calling up the head of the lab and asking for spare boards to be installed.

I looked around to make sure nobody else was present in the factory, glided swiftly to another computer of a similar kind standing in another corner, opened it, pulled out its memory boards, wiped my finger prints away with a handkerchief (well, not really!), slid over to my system, installed them, shut the panel, started up my machine.

All done and dusted before anyone could say "whoosh"; not that there was anyone else there at that time to say so.

I did track down the missing memory boards later. Apparently, one of our customer-support engineers had received an irate call at night from an angry customer whose computer had crashed in the middle of some crucial work.

Our engineer didn't really know what could have gone wrong, but he had come to the factory at 4 a.m., picked a few spare parts—among them were my memory boards—which he thought may come in handy.

Anyway, the demonstration was a glorious success. The customer went away happy. So my boss was happy. Everybody was happy—except one poor soul who was sulking in the other corner of the lab because the system on which he needed to run a benchmark the next day didn't seem to be working!

Sometimes—as in this case—such incidents happened inadvertently, but at other times these turned out to be deliberately planned adventures to pull somebody's leg.

Unlike the offices you see today, we didn't have access to a computer right on our desk—not even in TIFR which was far more liberal with resources than a company like Patni could afford to be. The most important room in the office was the "terminal room". There, on long benches lined with the wall, one would find a number of terminals connected to the computer which could be seen lurking in the adjacent room.

In order to do your work, you had to be clever enough to grab a terminal before anybody else did so, since there were never enough terminals for everyone. After finding one, you couldn't just sit in front of a terminal the whole day. First, the terminal room used to be icy cold and there was a distinct danger of getting frostbitten in your toes if you overstayed. Second, you couldn't eat or drink anything in the terminal room. And, you had to get up from time to time to answer nature's call anyway.

So even if you managed to grab a terminal early in the morning, you had to give it up after some time and wait for the next opportunity to pounce on one like a tiger waiting at a waterhole for a careless deer.

Two colleagues of mine—let us call them Subhash and Suresh—had rubbed others the wrong way by always pushing themselves in the terminal room before anybody else to grab a terminal. After many a foot were trampled upon by these two guys on numerous occasions, a plan was hatched to teach them a lesson. Early one morning, as usual, both had ruthlessly elbowed their way in the room, grabbed two terminals next to each other and started typing away on their keyboards.

Within seconds both halted with puzzled faces because the letters appearing on their screens weren't what they had typed! Both started typing a letter each at a time but clearly the letter appearing on their screen wasn't what they had typed. Suresh glanced at his neighbour's screen and realized that what should have appeared on his own screen was being displayed on Subhash's screen!

What was this black magic?

By then all of us were having a good laugh. "Do you need help, guys?" somebody asked.

The trick played on them was simple. The cables connecting the keyboards to the terminals ran under the table, and their entire length wasn't visible. So it was an easy matter to switch the position of the keyboards; and place Suresh's keyboard in front of Subhash's terminal and vice-versa.

The decades that followed after 1990 saw the Indian IT industry follow a very different trajectory—different from whatever I have so far described—to achieve spectacular success and growth. The cornerstone of this heady growth was the "industrialization" of the process of software production which the Indian IT companies brought about.

I would even venture to claim that this "industrialization" was as dramatic an achievement as, say, the transformation of the manufacturing industry in the last century by the invention of the assembly line.

Fortunately I happened to be present in the right place at the right time—purely by chance—when this exhilarating journey started. Being a part of it and a contributor to it has been a matter of some pride and a great deal of pleasure for me.

The wave that the Indian IT industry was to ride to dazzle the world later on had slowly started taking shape in the eighties.

In Patni, while most of my initial years were largely spent doing business with our Indian customers; the company had started developing software for customers in the United States.

If somebody had visited our office in Nariman Point during that time he would have seen few signs of this activity because most of the actual work was being carried out by our people spending time in the United States in our customers' offices.

The principles of this business were simple:

"You have a problem to solve Mr Customer from the US of A. You need to get this software developed in a short period of time. You aren't going to be able to find enough number of qualified people to do so very quickly, and even if you do so they will cost you an arm and a leg.

We have these genius Indian engineers with the best of training in all matters related to computers. They are available today, and they will cost you half of what you may need to pay locally. They can be here in your office in two weeks!"

The economics of such a proposition was compelling. The challenge lay more in convincing the customer that our people indeed had the ability, knowledge and training to contribute effectively to their projects.

An even bigger challenge was to convince the customer that we didn't have to do this work sitting in their offices. It could just as well be done sitting in our office in India—a few thousand kilometers and several time zones away.

The problem in claiming this with any degree of conviction lay in the unavailability of effective means of communications— something which we don't even think twice about today.

Developing large and complex software systems is as much a "social" activity as it is an engineering endeavour. In some sense the software engineer needs to read the customer's or the end-user's mind. Extract the unstated needs and desires of the customer and convert them into explicit statements on paper.

One could argue that the act of creating any new product must require the product developer to do exactly the same thing.

The difference and thus the difficulty is the intangible nature of software.

The specifications of a tangible product such as a house or a bridge or a car can be written down objectively and unambiguously in measurable attributes and properties of the product to be built. Prototypes or scaled-down models of such products can be built cheaply and quickly to convey with a great deal of accuracy how the final product will look and behave and what kind of experience the user may get when using the final product. It is possible to "scale down" such products without sacrificing the essential features and functions.

In case of software, the concept of scaling down does not really work well. Scaling down software usually implies removing features and functions and thus sacrificing the ability to convey accurately what the ultimate behaviour of the final version of the software system will be.

The customer or end-user therefore has to wait to fully comprehend whether the software meets all their needs and desires until the final product has been built. If some essential need has been missed, it is then too late or too expensive to provide for it at that stage.

A better strategy, therefore, is to be constantly in close communication with the customer so that you can understand their requirements and desires explicitly.

This challenge remains daunting even today with all that the modern-day communication systems have to offer. In the eighties and the nineties it was even more so due to the lack of means of effective communications such as internet, email, mobile telephony, video conferencing, instant messaging, which we take for granted today.

My first experience of working for a non-Indian customer came through a project we had won for an American company called Codex (the company does not exist anymore). This was a time when the Internet did not exist. There was no email, no world-wide-web, no browsers and certainly no social media. Technology to inter-connect computers in a large network so that they could exchange information, solve large problems collaboratively by pooling together their computing resources was just about being utilized outside research labs in industrial settings.

Codex at that time was designing such a network that was to be used to interconnect isolated airline reservation systems. Our role in it was to design and develop some of the software needed to manage such a complex, potentially world-girdling network.

I had worked on and had seen such things in TIFR and all my formal education in IIT was directly usable in something like this. This was an exciting project to get involved in. But the single-biggest problem in this project was "communication"—not the communication between the components of the network which Codex was building but the communication between us and them.

The primary means of sending information which both of us needed, back and forth, was a telex. This was a technology developed in the 1930s to supersede telegrams. Communication via a telex was just a little better than sending telegrams using Morse code!

You could only send text messages at the speed of 50 bits per second and had to wait for a reply till the next morning. In urgent cases one could make a phone call, but international phone calls needed to be booked in advance and were extremely expensive to make anyway. Since we were in different continents, sometimes we had to wait for as many as eight hours to ask a simple question.

The communication problem was creating too much pressure, because compared to what I had been doing for all our Indian customers this project was on a very different plane of engineering complexity and sophistication.

Luckily there was one factor which helped us. That was the customers' personnel with whom we were interacting.

They were as much, if not more, knowledgeable about technology, knew exactly what they wanted and were able to specify what they expected us to deliver.

Moreover, we were getting paid good money for developing "software"! Unlike most of the Indian customers, they valued this intangible product which we were building for them. It wasn't a freebie and our time, knowledge and effort were getting their worth. This was a new experience for me.

After Codex, as I got involved in more and more international projects, the world of computing—glimpses of which I had seen while in TIFR—started opening out again.

In this world, computers were being deployed for solving problems which couldn't be solved effectively without them—such as the Codex project. They were being used to improve productivity, efficiency and effectiveness of business processes and the people who executed them.

However, at that time, the number of people who directly interacted with a computer or who knew how a computer worked, how to program it to fulfil some purpose was relatively a minority even in the rich, developed world.

In a typical office an employee's routine still depended largely on files and papers, tortuously winding their way through the labyrinth of standard office procedures. Completing any task that involved several people working collaboratively, sharing information, commenting on each other's view, building a consensus was a time-consuming process. It is not because the people were inefficient or lazy but because the procedure took too much effort and time.

But around this time computers had started coming out of their glass-walled caves and were touching the daily lives of people. The "personal" computer was still undreamt of but access to computing power and tools had started appearing on an office worker's desk more frequently. This was the backdrop of a very interesting project I undertook in the mid-eighties.

A company called Applix, based in a town near Boston in the United States, was building a suite of integrated applications aimed at making the office paperless and creating a computer-aided platform to unclog and lubricate day-to-day office procedures.

The technology itself was not particularly esoteric. But the concept of automating routine office procedures so completely that no papers needed to cross over from one table to another was in itself very interesting.

In principle, you could throw your pens, writing pads, memos and files and bulky filing cabinets in the dustbin!

Instead you could use this suite of applications to create documents, memos and spreadsheets to crunch numbers and file them into an electronic filing cabinet, send them to your manager for review and approval, post messages which did not need to be routed through a mailman but could get delivered instantly in an electronic mailbox of your colleague. You could peep into the diaries (electronic) of your colleagues to find common free time for a meeting. It did not matter whether your co-workers were sitting next to you, in a different building or in a different city or continent.

All this is something you take for granted today because even your smartphone has such tools. At that time though it was a radical way leveraging the might of computers to ease the burden of man.

The other interesting thing about this project was that the people who were going to use this software everyday did not require any specialist computing knowledge, they did not even need to know that behind the keyboard which they would be hammering on all day, there was the most complex machine humans had ever built!

This project represented the broader trend emerging everywhere in the developed world. The presence of computers was slowly but surely becoming ubiquitous but at the same time completely invisible and intertwined in people's daily lives.

I spent about ten months in Applix's office in the US working on this project. Unlike Codex, this was a case where the customer wasn't comfortable with the idea of a team sitting in another continent developing software for them. This was ironical because, as I mentioned, the whole purpose of the software which Applix was building was to break the walls of a conventional office and make it possible for a team unfettered by distance to work together!

CHAPTER NINE

Culture Shocks

While I was getting exposed to international clients and their projects like Codex and Applix, the emerging Indian IT industry had started capitalizing on its basic business proposition—"We can do it cheaper and faster". It still had to prove: "We can do it better".

The opportunity clearly existed in the international arena, especially in the English-speaking developed world, which was inducting technology in more and more spheres of industrial processes at a faster and faster pace. They had the money to spend and the desire and market compulsions to increasingly use technology to innovate and grow.

A complementary situation existed in India. For a large number of parents in India, the illusion of upward mobility was closely tied with their children's fluency in English. The stamp of a university degree, especially in engineering, was firmly embedded in their psyche as the stepping stone to success.

These social aspirations were driving more and more kids to go through engineering schools, creating a pool of people with relatively limited opportunities commensurate with their intellectual (real or perceived) capabilities locally.

It wasn't surprising that someone put two and two together and created a thriving business out of it. IT companies had started sending plane loads of newly graduated engineers out to work on software projects to the US. For example, eight out of ten of my friends who had joined some IT company or the other at the time I joined TIFR were already in the US, and not for higher studies.

It has been argued that this was no more than indentured labour; no different from what had happened a century ago when ship loads of bonded labourers were sent from India to distant places like Jamaica, South Africa or Mauritius to work on sugarcane plantations or paddy farms.

In a purely philosophical discourse, this argument may be difficult to refute.

But this exodus of IT professionals was different for many reasons.

First, these "indentured" workers were eager to go where they were being sent.

Second, they were the intellectual equals of those for whom they were sent to work. They knew it and, more importantly, their foreign bosses knew it too.

Third, they were "hungry" for their own growth and quickly figured out how to progress from being just a "Hey, you!" to a valuable member of the project team.

The road to this state of affairs, and beyond to the real watershed that was to come, was strewn with many challenges, however.

One of the most interesting challenges, which sometimes resulted in embarrassing or hilarious or learning experiences, was essentially cultural.

As I mentioned earlier, software development is as much a "social" activity as it is an engineering process. To produce useful outcomes through social activities, people involved in them need to engage, communicate, respect and build relationships with each other. All of this becomes difficult when the individuals interacting with each other unknowingly bring different cultural baggage with them. Even simple things can become a hindrance in such matters.

For instance, for quite some time after I started working at Applix I would address almost everybody who looked older than me as "Mr XYZ". Every time I did so I would get a strange look from the person. Pretty soon I noticed that their interactions with me were very formal and noticeably distant. So one day, mustering courage, I drew my manager aside and asked him if I was doing something wrong. He said, "No. We like your work, but some people feel you are not very friendly!"

So next Monday, in a team meeting, I got up and said, "Guys, I am afraid I have started on the wrong foot. I have been conditioned to not call people older than me by their first name. For me it is a mark of respect and not unfriendliness".

Everybody had a good laugh and the matter was promptly forgotten.

A few years later, after we started exploring business opportunities in Japan, I was caught napping again. We were close to concluding an agreement to start our first-ever project for a Japanese company and I had gone to their office in Tokyo to discuss the technical details of the project.

Introducing yourself and exchanging business cards is a solemn ritual with a strict protocol (which I was unaware of then) in Japan. Having got past that without any apparent faux pas we sat down for a discussion.

I made some inconsequential remark about something to get the conversation started, addressing the leader of the customer's team (a very senior person) by his first name.

I thought I saw a flicker of disapproval on his face for a moment and was a bit puzzled. As the discussion progressed I realized ALL of them were addressing me as "Mr Joshi", but more importantly ALL of them were addressing each other also by their last name!

It was apparent that all of them had worked together for years, knew each other very well and yet in that meeting never once did I hear anyone being addressed by their first name.

I had to very quickly unlearn the Applix lesson to avoid putting my foot in my own mouth.

The trouble was that most of our customers in those days knew next to nothing about India and many of us didn't know that they knew nothing about our country. In fact, most of us had equally inadequate knowledge of their social norms, viewpoints and sensibilities.

It was imperative that we learned fast and consciously adopted and changed our behaviour depending on the person we were interacting with and where he/she came from.

But there were things nobody had any control over, and some embarrassing situations occurred.

It happened in the early nineties. We had just acquired our first customer in Germany and he wanted to visit our offices in Mumbai before giving the go-ahead to start work. Even for him, this was the first experience of working with a non-European software developer, and from his point of view he was also taking considerable risk by trusting us with this project.

I was to pick him up at the airport and drop him at his hotel. It was about 1:30 a.m., the busiest time at Mumbai airport; a few hundred or more people were glued to the barrier separating them from the arrival gate. With so many people talking, laughing, stamping their feet to ward off mosquitoes, the ambient noise level was near deafening, as it is usually anywhere in Mumbai.

Wilhelm looked overwhelmed by the crowd and the noise as he emerged from the exit because when I managed to hold his elbow and steer him through the crowd to the parking lot, there were beads of perspiration lining his forehead.

There was a more prosaic reason for the sweating. It was January and he was wearing an overcoat because he had assumed that Mumbai too would be in the middle of its winter. As we got into the taxi he shed his coat quickly and peering through the window, asked, "Is some VIP expected? Why is there such a big crowd?"

I said, "Yes, they have all come to receive you!" As he laughed, I explained that it was quite common in our country for the entire family, and sometimes friends too, to go to the airport to receive a guest.

The next day, he was at our office. We had a good meeting. The world inside the office was something he was used to. Probably our office was better appointed than his own office which was in an old red-brick building in a small town near Stuttgart, which used to be a warehouse in not too distant a past.

After a satisfactory meeting we started out for lunch. In the car he said, "This country of yours is stranger than I had imagined."

"What do you mean?" I asked.

"There seem to be two completely contrasting worlds co-existing in the same physical space. Inside the office—the people, the technology, the order, the discipline and the work culture—everything is as I would expect in a modern technology company anywhere in the world.

"The India outside is as chaotic, disorderly as I had imagined it would be. I even saw a cow or two this morning when driving from the hotel to your office, calmly weaving their way through traffic. In fact, I was told that I shouldn't be surprised if I saw an elephant on road."

"Elephant! Come on, now that is a bit of exaggeration…", I was just blurting this out when we turned a corner, and lo and behold, right in the middle of the busy road there was a procession with people chanting, banging on drums and cymbals around a decorated elephant with some deity on its back!

Wilhelm promptly fished out his camera and craning his neck out of the window started clicking photographs.

"See I told you," he said triumphantly, and I didn't know where to hide. I am sure he went back convinced that apart from rickety Fiat cars, designed in the 1940s, elephants on roads, too, were a commonplace sight in a city like Mumbai!

It wasn't just the business environment where these surprises lurked. People like me were spending long periods of time in foreign lands, were interacting with people inside and outside the office and were exposed to situations that had no parallel in their past experiences.

During summer, sometimes it can get quite warm even in the Boston area where I was living in an apartment for a few months. Due to the heat, the windows of the apartment would be open all the time. Usually I and my roommate would cook at home in the evenings—simple things—rice, dal and some vegetables.

One day in the evening, as we were climbing the stairs to our apartment, our neighbour accosted us and complained about the strong smells emerging from our kitchen which would reach his living room if our windows were open.

We weren't sure what to make of this. First of all, we were puzzled—why would somebody find the smells of all the wonderful spices we put in our food "offensive"? We were so used to the aroma of such spices back in India.

Second, we would never have even considered it appropriate social behaviour to go and complain to our neighbours even if they were frying dried Bombil (Bombay Duck) which are so "fragrant" that not just the immediate neighbours but the whole neighbourhood would smell them being fried.

Generally, a word like *culture* is associated with music, art, language, sports and history—the distinct and manifest aspects of a society. Understanding a different culture is, therefore, equated with learning about the history, art, language, sports, etc., of that different culture.

While undoubtedly that is necessary, that is the easy part because what you need to learn is obvious and materials and channels to do so are easily available.

The difficult part is to first notice the small and subtle peculiarities, unusual patterns of behaviour and beliefs that individuals display in everyday interactions and then learn to either adopt them or to at least clearly identify them.

It is not the obvious symbols of cultural differences but these small-little things that are more important to building relationships that can withstand such cultural differences—business or personal.

In Applix it would have been perfectly okay for me to ask: "Who is Larry Bird and why is he famous?" People around me would have happily taken the trouble to explain that he is the biggest star in the Boston Celtics basketball team and would have even taken me to see a Celtics basketball game so that I will learn to appreciate why they all were so crazy about him.

It was, however, not okay for me to call them by their last name or to forget to say "thank you" or "you are welcome" in situations where they expected it, but my native cultural background had never taught me to be alert to such subtleties. Moreover, nobody would have taken the trouble to explain this to me on their own. I had to take that extra step to correct my mistakes!

While dealing with customers in America, language, at least, wasn't a barrier. The first few forays in Japan presented completely different challenges. My manager Mr Godbole and I had gone to Japan to explore business opportunities.

We had a meeting with the chief technology officer of a large Japanese technology company. We had done our homework and research about this company. We had read everything that was available in public domain about their business and their products.

We thought we had a good idea about how to get them interested in our services. We had prepared a solid presentation, including case studies showcasing our expertise and experience of working with companies in America doing business in similar areas.

The meeting started and soon we realized that our prospective customer could not speak a word of English! Of course, neither of us could speak a word of Japanese!

This was strange because he had replied to my email in English!

The meeting looked like a complete wash out.

Before beating a retreat from his office, as a last-ditch effort, I got up and went to t white board. I drew a vertical line to divide the board in the two halves. At the top of the left half I wrote "Patni Computer Systems", and at the top of the right half I wrote the name of his company.

And whatever I was planning to speak as part of my presentation, I started writing on the left half of the board. I saw our host's face light up. I offered the marker pen to him. He got up and came to the board and the next one hour we spent alternately writing in our respective halves of the board, conducting a completely silent but very lively discussion!

Of course, this wasn't a very productive way of holding a discussion. Later, we always had either a professional interpreter or, as time went by, our own Japanese-speaking employees in every meeting in Japan.

As the IT business started changing from manufacturing computers for Indian customers to developing and maintaining software for international customers, a very different kind of cultural problem cropped up at home.

The business was assuming a shape that we today associate with IT Industry—that of a "service provider" (as opposed to a "manufacturer of products to sell").

A "service", by its very definition, needs to be provided when it is asked for.

A "product" can be manufactured in anticipation of its need and stocked in a warehouse to be delivered when asked for. A product manufacturer can therefore afford to follow his own schedule, keep his own timings as he sees it fit.

A service provider needs to be always ready to work to produce the service which cannot be stocked in anticipation of the demand; customer can demand it at any time of the day or night—seven days a week, twenty-four hours a day!

As the customer base of Indian IT companies started expanding globally, the concept of a "working day" became meaningless.

A customer in Japan would wake up three-and-half hours before we normally would, and a customer in California would wind up his workday six-and-a-half hours after we would normally have gone to sleep—just about the time the customer in Japan was starting his work-day! If we hoped to do business with both of them we had to make sure we were awake and in control of our faculties all the time!

It was a difficult task to explain to the family why on some days I had to leave for office at 5:30 a.m. (9:00 a.m. in Japan) or why, on some days, I would come home only after midnight (because there was an important discussion planned with a customer in California at 10:00 a.m.—his time).

My father used to leave home for work exactly at 9:00 a.m., and would be home just when the clock struck 6:00 p.m. His entire life and events were planned around this inviolate predictability. Pretty much everybody around me was living a similar kind of life, and people's presence in a certain place at a certain time could be predicted with certainty, weeks, if not months, ahead.

I couldn't even predict whether I would be home for dinner the next day, or whether I would be calling in to say not to wait for me to have dinner from some other city in some other part of the world!

In the absence of emails, internet, Skype and even reliable telephony, communicating with your family had to be treated like a software development project—planned in advance, executed to perfection.

During my first trip abroad, I would plan a certain time on a certain night to call my family. Since the government of the day considered making a telephone available to an ordinary citizen a great favour—something you had to plead to get after waiting for a decade—my family would gather around a phone at my sister's house, who was amongst the privileged few to have a phone.

Everybody would be waiting for his or her share of the few minutes that the call would last—which provided precious few moments to talk to my wife who had started calling herself a "Software Widow"!

Letters, which took weeks to reach, and sometimes never did, provided the only means of any private conversations.

Today the improved means and easy availability of fancy communication technology and gadgets haven't quite solved the problem. If anything, it has made it worse. Because the same technology places demand on your time even more than seven days a week and twenty-four hours a day, if such a thing is possible!!

CHAPTER TEN

From Artisans to Engineers

The "software exports" business of Indian companies started growing rapidly in the developed world—from Japan in the East to the US in the West. The backbone of this growth was the "export" of software engineers since customers abroad wanted the work to be done in their offices.

In response to that, IT companies in India such as TCS, Infosys, Wipro, Patni, Datamatics etc., were sending qualified engineers not just in hundreds but in thousands for "onsite" work.

In a situation where demand was outstripping supply, where lucrative payments in foreign currency were forthcoming literally upon being asked, where the engineers were as eager to go to Bloomington, Illinois, as they were loath to go to Mathura, U.P., there was no incentive for these IT companies to chase business in India.

Why would you pursue some company in Nagpur that wanted free software in return for buying your computers, a company that nitpicked for every paisa it paid you and where your employees were reluctant to go and work anyway?

Many companies like ours, which initially started with manufacturing and selling computers, split themselves down the middle—one part focusing exclusively on the software "exports" business, and the other continuing the hard work of selling computers in India.

Expectedly, the international business boomed while the domestic business chugged along as best as the conditions permitted.

But this "explosion" of the international business was not sustainable and scalable in the long term, at least not as long as it primarily depended on "body shopping". The logistics of transporting a large number of engineers to the US and other countries were challenging.

You had to find and hire qualified people at a rate faster than the demand for them. Visas had to be obtained from reluctant countries. People had to be convinced to get up and go to a foreign land for long durations at an instant's notice.

After having sent people on site you had to deal with all kinds of issues. Somebody would get bored and would want to come back, somebody wouldn't want to stay in California because it was too expensive, others would want to work only in California because it was the land of opportunity, somebody would want to return to India to attend a wedding!

Given the broad applicability of relations like "brother", "sister", "uncle", "aunt" and the emotions attached to various events in their lives (birth, death, marriage, thread ceremony, anniversary) in India, it would often become very challenging to explain to an American customer why it was important for a particular engineer to return to India.

Somebody's parents would come to our office and pester us to let their son or daughter—who was doing a project in San Diego—to return because they had heard of an earthquake in San Francisco! There were some who would start scanning "wanted" columns from the day of landing on foreign shores, and jump ship without notice—leaving behind an irate customer and creating a bad record for the company in the eyes of the visa authorities.

As long as the number was small, all of this could be managed but beyond a point, business was bound to suffer. As each "unmanaged" event of this kind had the potential to antagonize either our employee or the customer. The sustainability of this model was questionable in the long run.

To add to this complexity, the established companies had to deal with another headache. A number of so-called IT companies mushroomed all over India. Such a company would have one owner, one telephone—the owner doubling as secretary/telephone operator—with a name having some variation of the phrase "Information Technology".

They would lure engineers hungry for greener pastures or poach on the bigger IT companies. They would find some opening or the other in a company in the US through their personal contacts (my wife's uncle's in-law's nephew's Harvard classmate is a CIO in Acme Corp!) and send these new "employees" on subsistence wages.

These companies would be here today, gone tomorrow leaving both the employee and the customer in the lurch while maligning the reputation of the burgeoning IT industry in India.

Moreover, as these dubious companies demonstrated, the body-shopping model was essentially a commoditized business with the suppliers, i.e., the Indian IT companies, adding almost no value in the process other than being good at managing recruitment and travel logistics.

As a result, as any commoditized business would be, this business too was subject to price wars, had little or no entry barriers for more and more competitors to crowd the market, easy for customers to switch suppliers and sensitive to the whim and fancy of visa-policy changes.

For long-term sustainability of this business, the solution was obvious, at least in theory. Find a way to deliver "value" through well-defined "services" (and not just qualified people) from India.

One could think of many different ways by which "value" could be created. For example, value could be created by investing in your own intellectual property—

in the form of new products, technology, solutions which nobody else had created before.

However, this path, though rewarding if successfully traversed, was also full of crevasses. It required large upfront investments and deep pockets. It needed the ability to envision future opportunities and the stomach to gamble on them, and a dash of luck too!

Alternatively, value could also be created by adopting different techniques to improve the delivery of services—by increasing efficiency, quality and predictability or by reducing risks or a combination of one or more of these. A safer route, though less rewarding in the long run, this was the path that the Indian IT industry chose.

The Indian IT industry "industrialized" the process of software production and other services associated with the production of software.

One could argue that there was nothing radical in this. The same idea had already been used many a time in several other businesses. For example, as far back in the past as 1913, Henry Ford brought about a revolution in automobile production by doing something very analogous, i.e., installing a moving assembly line.

Historically, there was little difference between an artisan and a manufacturer. The quality, quantity, features/functions and value of a manufactured item—whether it was a chair or a car—depended on the experience, skill, creativity and productivity of the person (or persons) engaged in the act of making it.

The same product even when manufactured by the same person on two different occasions would not be identical. If two different people produced it, it would definitely be not the same. The differences may sometimes give the customer a pleasant surprise and at other times a dismal shock.

As long as the quantities to be manufactured were small, this state of affairs wasn't too bad. Since the satisfaction and loyalty of the customers was highly dependent on the skill levels of individuals employed to make the product, the manufacturing company would carefully screen the "artisans" it employed to make sure they had the highest levels of skills, experience and past references.

This model of running a manufacturing business wasn't, however, scalable to produce large quantities of a product with predictable quality and performance. There was a limit on how many such highly skilled artisans could be found and be retained. If one or more of them were lured away by a competitor, the customers who they served were likely to walk away to the competitor as well.

This was exactly the same situation that the Indian software industry was grappling with. The manufacturing industry extracted itself out of this situation by a simple trick. It is the power of hindsight that enables us to audaciously call it "simple" now. I am sure at the time this was being done it was an extremely large and complex change.

There were myriad tasks which needed to be performed to manufacture any moderately complex product. They were divided into two categories. One which required special skills, knowledge and creativity and the other which could be performed by practically anybody with a bit of training, practice and adhering to a strict discipline.

It was no surprise then that the bulk of efforts required to manufacture most products fell into the second category.

In one stroke, the need for special skills was stamped out of most of the activities and along with this was removed the risk of potential errors, omissions and variations which affected the quality of the manufactured product. With most of the individuals employed, performing the same task repeatedly day after day, their productivity saw a dramatic upswing.

How dramatic?

For instance, expanding on this basic idea and augmenting it with a moving assembly line, the Ford motor company reduced the time for assembling a complete car chassis from 728 minutes to 93 minutes. That is productivity improvement by a factor of eight. This brought the cost of a Ford Model T car down from about 1,000 dollars (in 1908) to less than 250 dollars a few years later. But that was not all, the company could afford to double the wages of its workers at the same time!

It wasn't as if the software industry and academia were not aware of or had ignored these lessons. An entire discipline called software engineering was devoted to bring about exactly this kind of change in the process of software development. Both the academicians and industry researchers had developed a plethora of techniques, tools, standards, books, papers and training programmes aimed at transforming software development from a creative art to an industrialized, repeatable and predictable process.

Most of the respectable IT companies in the world had even adopted many of these techniques and tools as a part of their standard-operating procedure.

What was then so unique about the Indian software industry?

The single-minded focus, devotion and discipline—almost bordering on fanaticism—with which the Indian companies adopted these software-engineering standards, models, techniques and tools was unprecedented. Equally unprecedented was the speed with which the adoption progressed and the scale on which it was carried out.

With the furious adoption of software engineering and quality frameworks such as the Capability Maturity Model developed at Carnegie Mellon University or embracing standards such as ISO 9000/27000 and the discipline that came with it, it became possible to induct into the work force even those who did not have specialist degrees in computer science or information technology. It became possible to make them productive quickly, with training and mentoring.

Dependence on an individual's ingenuity to produce high-quality software was replaced by tightly defined procedures, detailed specifications of tasks to be performed and enforcing adherence to internationally recognized standards.

It becomes possible to achieve something analogous to what you find at any construction site. You don't assemble a team consisting of only civil engineers and architects to construct a building. In fact, if you try to construct anything with such a team, in all probability, it will fail to build anything useful!

Instead, you assemble a team of one architect, one civil engineer and a group of construction workers. The construction workers don't need the knowledge which the architect and the civil engineer have, and the architect and the civil engineer don't need the skills that the construction workers possess.

Each person has a specific role to play and needs only the skill and knowledge needed for that role. If you are able to explicitly define the roles and the skills needed to perform those roles, are able to implement a tight process to closely coordinate the activities of each of the role holders that compliments each other's efforts, then the constraints on scalability and predictability appear not so daunting anymore.

The fanaticism displayed by the Indian IT companies in adopting the latest (at that time) and the greatest that the discipline of software engineering had to offer undoubtedly paid rich dividends; even beyond the companies' own expectations. But implementing these new methods was only half the battle won!

The other half of the battle was to market the real (and also imagined) "value" of this "new" way of working to the customers.

One had to convince the customers that:

(a) This new way of working would produce higher quality software regardless of the qualifications (and quality) of people employed.

(b) Regardless of where the work was carried out, whether under their noses or in India, the quality of output will be the same.

A new superstition was being created and the Software Engineering Institute of the Carnegie Mellon university was a godsend in helping the Indian industry (inadvertently, I may add) in making this superstition respectable.

Being stamped with an ISO-9000 or a SEI-CMM Level-5 certification quickly became a guarantee of quality for both the buyers and the providers.

But this was a half-truth and people like me would squirm every time we were required to pitch to some customer the virtues of "our systems". However, I guess, sometimes it is good to believe in the myths you yourself have created. Conviction is infectious and if you hypnotize yourself into being convinced of the truth of what may be a myth, you will succeed in hypnotizing others to believe in the same thing—at least for a while.

That is what the Indian IT industry managed to do. And they managed to do it so successfully that when a number of other countries—Mexico, Philippines, Ireland, Eastern Europe and, most notably, China—envious of the success of Indian IT Industry in gaining prominence, tried to emulate it, none achieved quite the same level of success.

Don't get me wrong!

The implementation of models like ISO-9000 or SEI-CMMI brought about a change in the process of software production and it came with enormous benefits. The change was necessary and the Indian IT industry was the first in the world to bring about this change on a truly large scale. So one should give due credit to the industry for doing so.

However, "these models alone are sufficient to produce great quality software" was the myth that the industry created and managed to sell it to the world. One should give them credit for the creative way in which they managed to do so as well.

The net result was:

A vibrant, growing, enormously profitable Indian IT industry that caused the world to sit up and take notice.

It created opportunities for educated youth in the country that were non-existent.

It brought first millions and then billions of dollars of foreign exchange to India.

It eventually prompted every big, high-technology company in the world to consider India as an investment destination, to set up their R&D centres.

It gave indirect employment to countless people, from chaiwallas and vada-pav sellers serving the night shifts of BPO centres, to construction workers building new IT parks, to transport operators providing fleets of buses and taxis to the growing IT workforce.

Most importantly, this was the first instance of a purely indigenously grown business being viewed with respect and envy by the business community outside India.

I feel enormously proud of being a part of this journey.

CHAPTER ELEVEN

Battles for Survival

All this change did not happen overnight. Nor was the business-as-usual suspended while these new systems and techniques were being adopted and marketed to our customers.

The daily struggle to acquire new customers, convince them to allow us to work in our offices in India instead of sending our engineers to their office abroad, went on as before.

There were two sides to this struggle—addressing our customers' perception about our credibility and addressing their concerns about the quality and availability of infrastructure in India. The first we could manage on our own. The second depended on being able to get something useful done from the hidebound bureaucracy that surrounded us. And that was the harder part.

We had our offices located in a special export processing zone (SEEPZ). Creation of SEEPZ (and other zones like that elsewhere) was a great initiative by the Department of Commerce. It certainly helped companies manufacturing and exporting electronic equipment to get established and grow rapidly by providing a number of facilities—duty-free imports of technology, simplification of import/export procedures, tax concessions on export income, etc.

But hidden under almost every velvet glove was an iron fist which could crush your finger in a routine handshake.

For example, we couldn't get anything from our customers or send anything to our customers through a courier company like Fedex or Blue Dart. We had to import or export everything through a defined mechanism that would take weeks to get even a single disk (a "floppy" disk in good-old days) in or out.

In a business when speed of response was counted in hours, if not minutes, two weeks to get a single tape wasn't acceptable. The sanctioned mechanism was fine for a company that was manufacturing and shipping power supplies or disc drives by container loads. It wasn't going to work for us.

A bigger problem was the valuation of our output. We had a constant struggle on hand to convince the authorities that a single tape that we wanted to export may contain software worth more than a container-full of transformers, which our neighbour in Seepz was shipping through a truck. And, on another day, we may be shipping a tape of the same size and weight but valued at one tenth the value of the last shipment!

Fed up with the ban on courier services, we decided that we would send and receive what we needed electronically. The availability and quality of telecommunications in the country had changed dramatically after the mid-eighties due to the creation of organizations like CDOT (Center for Development of Telematics) and a general (albeit grudging) acceptance in Delhi that the state monopoly and control over telecommunications was hurting businesses and common people alike.

So we were very hopeful that a major infrastructure hurdle which our customers perceived as an enormous risk in allowing us to do their projects in India could be overcome. Once again we did not see the iron fist in the velvet glove soon enough.

First of all, any electronic equipment which was to be connected to a telecom line had to be certified by the department of telecommunication.

Their published list of certified equipment was age old and outdated. So much so that one of our customers laughed when I told him the model number of the modem (a piece of equipment which must be connected to a telephone line and which converts data being sent by your computer into appropriate electrical signals which can be transmitted over the telephone line) which we were planning to buy. He told me that I will get this particular model only in an antique shop!

The catch was—we weren't allowed to import the newest and the best that the technology of the day offered. You won't believe this, but once, while I was trying to justify our need for modern equipment to a local officer in the telephone exchange, he remarked, "Such untested devices might burn our telephone lines."

I didn't know whether to laugh or cry because the truth was that half the world was using them without any such damage being ever reported.

We had to be able to send software and data back and forth between our computers and the customers' computers. DoT (Department of Telecommunications) had very graciously started allowing companies such as ours to rent long-distance private telecommunication lines, which would allow us to set up such a connection.

Remember, Internet did not exist then. We were trying to create our own private network instead. But there again was a catch. Someone in his wisdom had decreed that we should be allowed to only set up "point-to-point" connections which meant I could use this long-distance line to communicate with only one customer.

Did the authorities seriously expect a company to survive by doing business with only one customer?

DoT thought so.

Because when I met a very highly placed official in DoT to plead our case to allow us to set up such connections with many of our customers based in the US and the UK, I was told that it could not be permitted. If we needed to set up communications between multiple customers, it must be done from different offices, which are not in the same building—one point-to-point line per office was permitted!

When I asked 'why', I was told that if they allowed us to have multiple lines coming into the same office, we could tie them together and become a "network operator" and provide our customers the ability to communicate with each other and thus become a competitor to DoT!

We had enough trouble running our own business with all these asinine regulations to deal with. We weren't going to add to our headache by getting into uncharted waters of a "network operator"!

We were accused of the same thing (of being desirous of defrauding the state of telecom revenue) in another context. This point-to-point telecom line, which we were so graciously given, couldn't be used for anything other than data. For example, it was technically possible to connect this line to our PABX system in the office so that our employees working on the customer's project could use it to talk to their counterparts. This could have saved so much of hardship and effort because software development is a collaborative activity where multiple people and teams have to communicate closely and constantly.

But no, again the bogey raised was that we could misuse this facility then to run a telephone service of our own and rob the nation of long-distance telephony revenues!

To be sure, there was a possibility of frauds and misuse. Technology doesn't by itself necessarily side with the honest and the righteous. The hands that wield it decide whether to use it for honest goals or for nefarious purposes.

But because something can be used in dishonest ways does not mean the technology itself should be outlawed. What that means is one should create systems and procedures that will allow honest people to use it to its fullest potential and the thieves, who wish to subvert it, could be caught and punished.

Doing that is hard work. It is so much easier to just not let progress happen so one does not have to worry about its consequences.

In other words, while there was immense progress in upgrading the technology of telecommunications in the country, the mindset of those in power had not changed one bit. The mindset that the industry was basically a bunch of crooks who would grab the first opportunity to rob the nation naked hadn't changed.

Whatever the industry did to become competitive in the world by constantly changing, acquiring new technology, adopting new methods and techniques, it still had to work its way through the labyrinth of archaic rules and regulations and power-hungry mandarins who tried to control its destiny.

What was even more galling was that despite all that control and power nothing was really being offered in return. We had to pay for the telecommunications facilities through our noses (at that time the cost of similar facilities in the developed world was at least three times less than what we were paying) but had no consumer rights to demand a minimum quality or availability of service.

Nobody could predict whether the service would be available or broken down on a given day. No business could live with this sort of uncertainty. We had to have two linesmen from the local telephone exchange almost on our payroll, just to ensure, that our telecommunication facilities worked at all times!

While this—sending software and data electronically to our customers—addressed a major hurdle in convincing our customers that we could sit in India and develop software almost as effectively as we could in their office, it created a different headache.

As I mentioned, at that time one of our bigger offices was in SEEPZ. Everything that we produced there was expected to be exported in exchange of foreign currency. The SEEPZ commissioner's office oversaw all the transactions which were carried out by all the companies in the zone.

In return for the various facilities which were made available to the companies operating in the zone, each company also had to fulfil some obligations regarding the amount of dollars they brought back in the country as a result of their exports. The problem was that companies such as ours earned dollars in three ways.

First, the fee that was paid for the services delivered by our employees by working at the customer's office. Was this an "export" done from SEEPZ? All of these employees were based in our SEEPZ office. So one could argue that any fees which were paid for their activities should be deemed as earned by our SEEPZ office and thus should get counted towards the export obligations which we had to fulfil. This, however, was a grey area for which nobody, including the government officials posted in SEEPZ, had any answer.

Second, we sat in our SEEPZ office; using our private network, we connected with the computers installed in our customer's offices in America or Canada or the UK and developed software directly on their computers. In a way, nothing was "sent" or "exported" from SEEPZ to another country except our keystrokes on the keyboard and via these key strokes our thoughts, brain-power, ingenuity and problem-solving ability. We were paid rather handsomely for these activities. But did it qualify as "export" within the letter of the law as it was understood by the authorities? Again, no one had an answer to this because no one had really expected "services" as opposed to tangible "goods" to be an exportable commodity. In fact, that sentence itself is an oxymoron. Service, by its very definition, is not a commodity!

Third, we sat in our SEEPZ office, developed software on our computers and sent it electronically over to our customers almost instantaneously. This should have fulfilled all the criteria of an "export" laid down in the rules which governed SEEPZ. We worked in our office, we produced something and we sent it to an overseas customer and we got paid in dollars in return. However, there was one thing missing. No one actually saw anything tangible being put in a package, sealed in the presence of a SEEPZ official, loaded onto a truck and sent under guard to the airport to be shipped as a consignment through some airline to a foreign country. How could then anybody believe that something was actually exported!

Every time we went to the SEEPZ office to submit our documents related to our "exports" there would be a debate and confusion all around. Were we actually exporting anything at all? Even if we were, how could we prove that the value of what we had exported was in fact what our documents claimed it to be? Or were we involved in some unsavoury activity and all this business of software export was only a façade?

In private, all of these officers would admit that in the first place the rules were archaic and short-sighted and second, they had not received any orientation, briefing or clarification about how to apply these rules to a business such as software development.

Finally, getting tired of these regular skirmishes both sides came to an undocumented understanding. We would faithfully copy some software which we were developing on to a couple of tapes every month, pack them in a box and "export" them to America. Since now there was physical package, it could be inspected and sealed by the concerned officers and sent through the officially sanctioned channel of airline shipments.

What the tapes contained they never asked, and we never told them. A win, win for both! Well, most of the time. Once in a while some new guy would come and the old fights would ensue.

Once as I was just about to leave for home when I got a frantic call from our administrative officer. He had gone to the SEEPZ office to clear a package that was sent by one of our customers from the US. The customer had sent some software which we urgently needed in order to complete our part of the project.

Since SEEPZ did not allow overnight couriers such as Fedex or DHL that package had to be sent through an airline shipment and had already been in transit for more than a week. The customer had sent the software on a tape of a new kind and the officer wasn't ready to release it because he wasn't convinced that what the documents claimed to be a tape was really a tape.

It looked like a rectangular box and not a round spool which is what tapes usually looked like in those days. The officer was convinced that we were smuggling in something valuable and were trying to pull wool over his eyes.

So I took a screw driver and went to the SEEPZ warehouse. Unscrewed the cover of the "box" and showed him the tightly wound tape—just as round as he wanted a tape to be! And finally, we were allowed to take the tape.

Our whole industry was so new and contained so many new things, which even we would at times find surprising, that such disagreements with the officialdom were inevitable.

However, there was something I used to find very puzzling then, and continue to find it baffling to this day.

Whenever a government officer in a position of power came across something he had not seen before, experienced something he had not experienced before, the first reaction invariably was to assume that we were guilty of something until proven otherwise. I don't know why there was such mistrust—was it because they had only dealt with deceitful people from our own community in the past? Or was it because the official dogma, being propagated by the political philosophy of the day, considered trying to run an honest business to be an impossible contradiction? I guess, I will never know.

Now, when I look back at these incidences, I wonder whether instead of getting upset, it may have been more prudent to offer to educate the people concerned about this new technology. After all, almost none of them had any relevant knowledge or training. Few of them had ever seen a computer before. They were just trying to cope with an unknown field and do their job in an environment where they knew they were out of their depth, but still had to exercise their authority. Perhaps with a little extra effort we might have made it a little easier for them. I guess that too is something I will never know.

Over the next few years things changed, and changed dramatically.

Instead of telling us why we were not allowed to do something, the officialdom started talking to us about how to solve the problems while staying compliant with the regulations.

There was a surge of regulatory changes. For example, an organization called Software Technology Parks of India (STPI) was set up. STPI made it possible to enjoy (almost) the same benefits of a special export zone like SEEPZ, while operating from practically anywhere.

Somebody knocked some sense into the telecom regulators and, suddenly, communication bandwidth was available for the asking with many of the strange and logic-defying restrictions being scaled back. Industry bodies like NASSCOM had a large role to play in convincing the bureaucracy of the huge potential that the IT industry had.

By the late nineties, the IT Industry had not only become the apple of every Indian's eye but it had also started challenging international IT powerhouses in their own backyard.

It led to the beginning of a reverse flow.

Until now we were travelling to foreign lands to develop software for our customers in their offices. Now the multinationals started considering the possibility of setting up their engineering and software development centres in India. All of a sudden, getting software developed and maintained in India—through an Indian company such as ours or by setting up their own offices in India—was starting to become a planned business strategy for even large multinationals like General Electric or Motorola or Siemens.

Just about then a big opportunity from an unexpected source presented itself for the Indian IT companies to rapidly scale up. This was (what eventually turned out to be the most-celebrated false alarm in human history) the tsunami of Y2K.

CHAPTER TWELVE

Tsunami or Windfall

December 31st, the last day of every year, is a cause of celebration the world over. Toasts are raised, kisses exchanged under the mistletoe, parties thrown, lights lit to ring in the New Year. The last day of the year 1999, however, was different.

While people usually stay awake on the night of 31st in hopeful anticipation of a glorious new year, in 1999, people in the developed world had lost their sleep in trepidation. They were fearful that some unprecedented doom was going to strike and turn the world upside down when 1999 turns to 2000.

What was this calamity that was expected to be bigger than the biggest of cyclones, tornadoes, cloudbursts, earthquakes, tsunamis and even El Nino? This was the Y2K problem, as it became known later, or the millennium bug.

The fear-mongering about this impending disaster had started much earlier.

As far back as in 1958, Bob Bemer, then working for IBM, had noticed a problem with the way dates were being represented in computer programs. He spent the next twenty years trying to convince IBM, the US government and the International Standards Organization to come out with guidelines for representation of dates in electronically stored information. Hardly anyone took him seriously then.

It was only in the nineties that the world suddenly woke up and took notice. By then so much of software had been written and computers had become such an integral part of the operations of the developed world that any thought of even the slightest disruption of this established order was nightmarish. Especially because no one really had an estimate of just how pervasive the problem was and which all systems and programs had been affected by it.

As a result, imagination ran wild.

The media was circulating all kinds of doomsday scenarios, at times even supported by eminent people in the position of power in the government, industry and academia.

It was predicted that when the clock would strike midnight on 31st December 1999, all computers, all over the world, will malfunction. Every activity that was controlled by or was dependent on these computers would come to a grinding halt.

Planes in the air will nose dive, trains on the tracks will derail, machines on the shop floor will stop, people in elevators will be stranded mid-floors, financial markets will collapse because banks will not be able to process any transactions, the list of potential problems was endless...

Everyone agreed that a potentially disruptive problem existed, but no one knew where it was and what effect, if at all, it would have.

What exactly was the problem? We have to go back to the sixties to understand that.

In those early days of computing, the memory of a computer, in which information was stored, was scarce and fearfully expensive. A computer with 8 kilobyte of memory was considered very respectable. And if someone wanted to buy a computer with a memory of 16 kilobyte, such a proposal was quickly rejected by the chief financial officer as unwarranted expense!

The worth of a programmer was measured by how economically he used the available memory and found ways of cramming more and more data in smaller and smaller memory banks.

In this environment, it was inevitable that storing a date as 21-11-1961 would be considered a fearful waste of memory as compared to storing it as 21-11-61 which served the purpose just as well. After all, we all knew what century we were living in, didn't we? So why waste precious memory in storing "19" when everybody could infer that 61 meant 1961! This was the mechanism used for decades by programmers, in billions of lines of software they had written all over the world (well not quite all over the world, but I will get to that later). How much of computer memory, and thus money, this practice would have saved in the decades that this practice was prevalent?

Well, no one had really attempted a calculation. However, given that at least in the developed world hundreds of thousands of computers running hundreds of millions of software programs—driving every conceivable commercial activity—were operational, the collective saving must have been considerable.

The consequence of this system of representing dates in the computer's memory was that on 31st December 1999, i.e., 31-12-99, after midnight all computers in the world would calculate the new day to be 01-01-00 and interpret it to mean 1st January 1900 and not 1st January 2000, as they should. This would lead to absurd calculations and wrong conclusions and the halting or malfunctioning of all processes, which depended on the correctness of these calculations.

The problem was that no one had thought that the programs written in the 1960s or 1970s would still be in active use thirty or forty years later. And no one had the foresight to imagine what would happen to the functioning of the programs when the year 1999 turned into the year 1900 as far as these computers were concerned (instead of turning into the year 2000).

Since the earliest computers were pressed into service, in the next four-odd decades, computers had invaded practically every industrial and financial activity—at least in the developed world. Therefore, a stoppage of everything from banking transactions and power generation to production in the factories and running railways and airlines would mean the whole of the developed world coming to a disastrous halt. That was the theory. Of course, come 1st January 2000 and the answer would have been known, but no one wanted to wait that long. Everyone also agreed that it was better to be safe than sorry!

The developed world went into a tizzy. Every conceivable business house lit fire under the chairs of their IT folk to try and find out whether and by what quantum their operations were likely to be affected.

But here was the problem—buried deep within millions of lines of software code, which they were using, were fragments of code written fifteen, twenty or even thirty years ago by people who had since quit the company or retired or had kicked the bucket. And these dear departed had left very little information or documents behind, explaining what they had done and where whatever they had done may be hidden in these millions of lines of code. This was like searching for the proverbial needle in a haystack!

Short of examining every single line of code, there was no known method of figuring out where exactly the problem lay and even after doing just that there was no known method of making sure that every single needle in the haystack had actually been found and removed! Doing so manually would mean pressing into service armies of programmers many times more in numbers than all the developed world could find.

The less-developed countries in Asia or Africa weren't too perturbed by this bogie because their dependence on computers to run their day-to-day lives was minimal. This was a mouthwatering opportunity for them to supply the manpower required to find and fix this problem—something they had in abundance.

But this wasn't just a game of numbers and population size. This wasn't digging ditches by the roadside which any able-bodied man could do. This needed qualified programmers. Only one country at that time had those in large numbers—India!

There was really only one sure-fire way to fix the problem—search every line of the programs to identify where a reference to a date expressed as six digits (ddmmyy) existed. Then change that line using eight digits' representation of dates (ddmmyyyy). Also, change every line where any manipulation of the date was being done to use the eight-digit representation and pad every stored record in every stored file or data base which contained a six-digit date with two extra digits, i.e., 19. After having done so, test every program with every such stored file or database to make sure that everything was working correctly.

Even the Indian IT companies collectively—large as they were—did not have the requisite number of programmers to do this manually. So several companies mushroomed, pedalling software tools to automate the detection of the occurrence of six-digit dates by scanning the programs.

All Indian companies swung into action. Finding business wasn't the problem. Coping up with the demand by mobilizing more and more programmers was the real challenge. Everyone was convinced that they had a problem and the paranoia was all pervasive. This paranoia would often land us into very illuminating situations.

There was this customer who came to us. His company had a sophisticated security system installed in their office which controlled the locks on the doors and the movement of lifts in the office. The doors would open automatically when an employee flashed her card, and the lifts would permit them to get off only on the floors they were supposed to work on.

These guys were convinced that unless something was done their smart system was going to fail and they were going to get locked out of their offices or get trapped in the lifts! Huh?

We were wondering why there should be such a panic about their locks and lifts. But hey, who were we to complain? They wanted us to check if there was a Y2K problem with their security software and were willing to pay good money for it!

As it turned out, their software remembered the date on which the last preventive maintenance activities were done (potentially different dates for each lock or lift) and automatically scheduled the next maintenance three months from that date. If the maintenance wasn't actually carried out on or before the scheduled date on a particular lift the software would shut down that lift until the maintenance activities were carried out.

Now the fear was that while calculating the next scheduled maintenance date if that date turned out to be a day after 1st January 2000, the software would interpret the scheduled maintenance date to be some day in the year 1900, i.e., it would mistakenly conclude that for nearly one hundred years no maintenance had been done! And thus shut everything down.

The scenario was theoretically plausible. Until then even we had not realized how insidious and obscure the Y2K problem may turn out to be. We were generally amused by the concerns and the amount of money and effort our customers and prospects were prepared to spend.

While this effort to remedy the Y2K situation was going on—on a war footing—there was a very different kind of eye opener in store for us.

We were in Japan, hunting for business. We had had some measure of success in snagging customers to do Y2K remediation work from the US and already had some successful projects under our belt. We had assumed that wherever in the world computers were being used and were critical to the economic activities in that country, there must exist similar opportunities for us.

We were confident that even a technologically developed country like Japan would be no exception.

The meeting began, and we went into our Y2Kservices pitch with full gusto. We went into details of how well-crafted our Y2K remediation processes were, how efficient we had made them by utilizing several effort-saving, automated tools, etc.

Everybody was listening with rapt attention. A question or two were asked about various technical aspects. After I stopped for a moment, everybody looked at each other and a smile slowly bloomed on our main customer's face. For a moment we were taken aback. He became solemn again and said, "I am very sorry for smiling, but we have no such problem and need no help".

My surprise at this blunt statement must have been very obvious, as he explained, "Look, most programmers in Japan have historically used a very different technique for saving memory space for storing dates. Dates, especially years, are stored as the number of years elapsed since the current emperor of Japan ascended to the throne. And since no emperor's reign has lasted longer than 99 years, we never have to worry about crossing over into a new century while projecting future dates!

For example, if a new emperor starts his reign on 4th May 1953. That day will be stored as 040501 and if the last day of his reign was 7th September 1975 then that day will be 070922. Ergo, we have no Y2K problem as you have called it."

So, in the end, we learned something new at the expense of a wasted trip to Japan.

Anyway, finally the dreaded night of 31st December 1999 came and the world waited with baited breath for the disaster to strike at midnight. What happened next was a complete anti-climax. Apart from a few inconsequential malfunctions of computerized systems nothing much was reported by the vigilant press. The most notable incidences were:

- In Australia a couple of bus ticket-vending machines had stopped working.

- In Delaware, in America, slot machines on a horse-racing track had stalled.
- In France the national weather bureau's website reported the date as 01-01-19100 in some obscure corner of a page.

No real disasters were noted, no plane crashed, no train derailed, nobody was even trapped in a lift, no power outages, no water-supply problems... absolutely nothing.

Was that because the millions of dollars spent on vigilance and preventive measures actually managed to avert the disaster? Hardly. Because despite the frenzied efforts only a small percentage of ALL existing software in the world was actually examined and modified in the available time and with the available manpower!

However, the Indian IT Industry had a windfall. And a comment or two is warranted about what exactly this windfall was.

The Indian IT companies saw a sudden spurt in their revenues because of this extraordinary surge of demand for their services. But that was not the real windfall. The relationships built with customers while executing the Y2K-remediation projects became the platform for many years of continued growth in business after the crisis blew over.

In the absence of this crisis situation, many of these relationships may never have been built in the first place. The Indian IT companies managed to solidify this customer base and utilized the goodwill to get deeper and deeper into the these organizations to diversify into all other core areas of IT work for these customers for many more years to come.

Indian companies which were until then fringe players in the IT-services market utilized this opportunity to become the mainstream suppliers of a diversified portfolio of IT services to their customers.

That was the real windfall.

CHAPTER THIRTEEN

New Horizons

The non-event called Y2K was a fortuitous shot in the arm of the Indian IT companies. And, they grabbed this opportunity—to forge relationship with large enterprises in the Western world—with both hands. These relationships fuelled the next surge of growth in the Indian IT industry.

These ties led the Indian IT companies to develop, maintain and manage software applications covering the entire business operations of big enterprises. Outsourcing software development and applications management to Indian IT companies became an integral part of the business strategy of many companies abroad. These companies were from a wide spectrum of businesses. There were manufacturers of every conceivable product—from shaving blades to computers, lipsticks to medicines and musical instruments to railway engines. These also included financial institutions, insurance companies, hotel chains, tour operators, TV and cable companies, besides gaming and gambling operators (where such businesses were legal).

Regardless of the business sector, information technology was crucial to them to make their business operations efficient, agile, and risk and error free.

We didn't necessarily understand or needed to understand their business processes in detail. We didn't understand what their customers wanted from them and what kind of products and services they needed to create and sell to become successful in their business. What we brought to the table was the skill to develop and manage software efficiently, quickly and cost-effectively.

In a broad sense, our contribution to our customer's business then was in enabling them to drastically reduce the cost of their operations, to increase the speed and efficiency of their business processes, to make it possible for them to change and reengineer their business processes quickly in the face of demands from their customers or competitive pressures.

Whether that made their customers happier, caused their customers to buy more of their products and services or helped them acquire new customers was hidden from us.

All this was great.

We were spreading our presence in our customers' operations, my company was growing, increasing its profits and signing up new customers. And, along with the company, I was growing. Instead of spending time developing software, I was mostly on a plane flying to Japan or America to sign up a new customer or to pacify an irate customer whose project had got delayed because of my team's mistakes.

I distinctly remember a day which started with breakfast in Warsaw in Poland, lunch with a customer in Malmo in Sweden, afternoon tea in Copenhagen in Denmark and dinner in London with another client.

Anju, my wife, had started believing that I come home only to get my clothes washed!

It was certainly exciting to interact with people from diverse cultures, learn about business practices in different countries, visit interesting places and try different cuisines, from that of Laplanders to Maoris.

But, on another level, it had started becoming a bit boring. Whether the materials-management software that my team was developing was for a tractor manufacturer in Japan or an electric razor manufacturer in Germany, it was in effect the same. Whether the customer was a life insurer in America or an automobile insurer in

Australia, the fraud-management software they wanted was essentially the same.

I was still an engineer at heart. I had spent seven years in IIT, learning hard to be an engineer. During my travels and interactions with our customers I had seen the exciting ways in which computers and computing technology was being used to engineer innovative products and systems that were making a positive impact on the lives of their users.

I had to find an outlet for this craving and find business opportunities in newer areas. I had started a small group in Patni with two of my colleagues, Ajay Chamania and Ashwin Gayatri, who were also bitten by the same bug—to explore potential opportunities which were closer to being called "engineering" in the classical sense of the word.

And things started clicking after many blind alleys and wrong turns.

I went for what I thought was a routine meeting with a small organization called National Milk Records (or NMR) in the UK. It was an eye-opening meeting.

They were doing something I had never heard before. The organization's primary business at that time was that of an advisor and provider of IT solutions to the dairy farms all over the UK. The primary goal was to help the dairy farms increase their output—both milk and meat.

They had been tracking data about the animal and milk production on these farms for more than twenty-five generations of the farm animals (primarily cows and bulls). They had complete family trees going back twenty-five generations of cattle with records of what these cows were fed, what were the ingredients of the feed, which cow and bull produced how many calves, which calves matured and gave how much milk during their lifetime, whether they were affected by any disease and what medicines were given to them, and so on and so forth.

The objective of collecting all this information was to analyse it and find correlations between feed, genealogy and milk production, and using such correlations tailor the feeding and breeding of the cows to increase milk production.

We knew how to write software to analyse large volumes of information, find patterns and correlations in that information. However, without knowing the meaning of that information and the objective of that analysis how were we to determine if our software was finding useful patterns and correlations.

This, of course, is the usual challenge for any information-technology practitioner. That is what makes software engineering such a challenging endeavour. Every time you think of developing a new software system, you have to begin by asking why you are thinking of developing it in the first place.

My team had to first spend enough time learning about dairy farming!

While this project was progressing—with some of my team working in the UK with NMR's experts and the rest designing and developing the software in India—we learned about another, even more, interesting possibility.

The question asked of us was: What kind of technology could we create to uniquely identify an individual cow, bull and calf? Traditional barbaric methods like branding were a no-no in a modern, more-enlightened world. And even if such cruel methods were used, they wouldn't have served the purpose anyway because in order to read the sign branded on the cow's rump, you have to first catch the cow.

What was needed was an instrument which could identify a cow uniquely, and instantly make available some basic information about the bovine to the farmer from a distance.

This unique identification was becoming critical for many reasons, including improving the collection and accuracy of the data which our software was to analyse. But more importantly because of an unrelated event which had caused a great deal of concern all over Europe at that time.

Around the nineties there had been an outbreak of the mad cow disease in the UK. This disease attacks the nervous system of the affected animal wherein the nervous system, including the brain, of the animal literally dissolves. Thousands of animals on the farms all over the UK had died because of this disease and around forty-five lakh animals had to be culled.

Since beef is an important part of the British diet, there was a considerable concern over meat from such diseased animals getting on to the dinner plates in restaurants and homes in the UK. Though there was no evidence found that eating the affected animal's meat would cause a human being to get affected, nobody wanted to take the risk.

There was, hence, a move to implement a system capable of tracing every piece of meat being sold in the market or being served in a restaurant back to the specific animal it came from. This was impossible without effective means of uniquely identifying every animal during its lifetime on a farm.

But what kind of technology could be used to identify an animal uniquely from a distance, and would allow the user to record additional information about the animal, tag it to the unique ID and automatically send it to the central database for recording?

The designed tool had to be light in weight, easy to carry and something that wouldn't interfere with the normal tasks of the user of the tool. It had to be designed such that it wouldn't cause pain or scare the animal. It had to withstand the rough and tumble of a typical farm environment—dust, rain, heat and sweaty palms of its user. Moreover, the tool couldn't cost an outrageous amount.

My heart gladdened at the prospect of this challenge. This was "true" engineering—working under seemingly impossible constraints and finding an innovative solution. This was one of those rare times where we had been exposed to the needs, wants and constraints of our customer's customer and had to design a product that was going to impact the end user.

It was decided to use a technology called RFID (Radio-frequency Identification). RFID had just begun to be used in many different situations which required accurate identification and traceability of movements of a product.

For example, in large retail store chains tracing the movement of goods is quite complicated. Goods are carried from the manufacturing plant to the warehouses and from there to the shelves of the retail stores. Here they are kept, until they are sold and carried out of the store. RFID had begun to be used to track the good through this entire path.

Traditionally, bar codes, which we all are familiar with, had been in use for such applications. However, RFID provided capabilities which bar codes could not.

The RFID technology consisted of essentially two components. The RFID tag—this was an extremely inexpensive and tiny (smaller than a grain of rice) electronic chip which could store a small amount of information. Second, the RFID reader, which could read the information stored in the tag from a distance without actually touching the tag.

For NMR, we designed a small clip-on gadget, which contained the RFID tag and which could be clipped on an animal's ear the moment the animal entered the farm—either because it was born on the farm or was bought by the farm.

Each tag would contain a unique number which would be used to identify the animal. The tag was also capable of carrying a small amount of other information about the animal temporarily.

We also designed a hand-held device; something that looked like a plastic toy gun which contained the RFID reader. This device could be clipped to the belt of the farmer. It was rugged enough to withstand the vicissitudes of the outdoors.

All afterthe farmer had to do was to aim it at an animal from a distance and click a button to read the contents of the tag on the animal's ear. The device had a small keyboard using which the farmer could enter additional information and connect it with the animal's unique ID.

The device could be connected to a computer when the farmer returned home after the day's work. Once connected, the software on the computer would read all the information that the device had gathered during the day and send it to NMR's central computer system for further processing.

Once this primary system was developed it could be applied in many different ways.

For example, the RFID reader could be integrated with the weighing machines on which the calves were being weighed periodically to track their weight. This information could now be automatically gathered. Also when the animals were given vaccines, the information could be recorded automatically.

We had given the farmers the magic wand of computing technology to free them of the painful drudgery of maintaining ledgers and notebooks!

This was a completely different world for us—instead of talking about production planning and balance sheets and insurance claims and investment banking, my team was debating whether there was a causal relation between some type of grass and quality of milk.

On my way to office I would pass through Aarey colony at Goregaon in Mumbai every day. While looking at the rows of buffalos chewing their cud I used to wonder when would technology—such as that which we were developing for NMR—be seen there. NMR was already planning to sell the technology to farms in far-flung places like Argentina.

However, despite all that highfaluting technology, there were a few things which they had to learn from us! One day Mark Usher, the in-charge of the technology in NMR, and I went for dinner in a small restaurant in Mumbai. Mark was a remarkable person—adventurous where food was concerned, a good cook himself, always ready to try something new and then go back home and cook it himself.

This was a restaurant specializing in the coastal food. Mark gorged himself on the spicy fish while wiping his brow. After dinner I asked for the menu to order desserts and saw "*kharwas*" on the menu. It is a rare delicacy made from the first milk that a cow produces after giving birth to a calf.

I ordered it, but didn't tell Mark what it was. Delicately flavoured with saffron and cardamom, Mark just loved it.

I told him, "If you can't tell what it is made of, you aren't fit to be an advisor to dairy farms. This is so connected with your profession".

"Connected with milk!" Mark said in disbelief. "I have eaten and drank everything that can be made anywhere on earth from milk. This can't have something to do with milk".

I had a hearty laugh and explained what it was made from. "I would never have believed it! In the UK, after the calf has had its fill, if there is any milk left over, it is just wasted because it is considered not fit to drink!" he told me.

I said, "See, here is a new business idea for you. You could generate some extra revenue for NMR!"

I don't know whether Mark ever followed up on my unsolicited advice!

CHAPTER FOURTEEN

Widening Horizons

The experience of working with NMR on their applications for dairy farming was exhilarating and different than the rest of our mainstream business. There was no doubt that this mainstream business was critical to putting butter on our bread. But there were surely these kind of challenging "engineering" projects available if only we kept actively looking for them while treading the beaten path.

And something completely different did come our way.

Remember, we are talking of the time before the proliferation of digital music devices such as iPods or online digital music stores like iTunes or smartphones like iPhones, capable of storing thousands of music tracks. CDs still ruled the roost and CD players were the dominant device on which the young and the old played their music.

The problem that everybody was constantly complaining about in this scenario was that the unit of purchase was a full CD containing anything from 12 to 18 or sometimes more songs. Out of these you loved some and hated some but were forced to shell out your hard-earned money even for the tracks you didn't like to be able to have those which you loved.

We came across a Japanese company which was in the process of creating a solution to address this problem.

The idea was to create a vending machine for music.

Japan was and is big on vending machines which sell everything from cola, hot and cold coffee, beer and cigarettes, fruit juices, tea, chocolates, peas laced with wasabi—practically anything which you can think of will be found in a vending machine.

In a city like Tokyo you cannot walk more than 100 feet in any direction in any part of the city without coming across a vending machine of some kind.

So why not a vending machine for music, where one could listen to a song, purchase it by inserting coins or notes in the vending machine and burn a customized CD containing only the songs which one liked.

The idea was brilliant. Moreover, this company wanted to connect all the vending machines into a single network so that they all could download songs from a central repository of unlimited songs.

The vending machines themselves were being designed by our customer. Our role was to design the software required for controlling the operations of the vending machine.

While we completed our task, and the engineering of the system itself was completed as planned, as far as I know, this was never successfully launched in the market.

Perhaps the company was grappling with issues of copyright with the owners of the music and couldn't come to an amicable arrangement. We never really knew, and there was considerable disappointment that an innovative system which we had worked hard to develop never saw the light of day.

While more and more opportunities for getting involved in such out-of-the-ordinary applications of computing technology were becoming available, there was a debate raging inside my company.

Doing this kind of work required a different set of skills, different processes, tools and knowledge and sometimes different kind of people.

Like, in case of the vending machine although we were not designing the machine itself, we needed to understand the designs. The software which we were to build was just one small component within a much bigger system and had to directly control the operations of that system. This meant we needed in our team engineers with mechanical and electronics engineering background who could also develop software.

All this translated into investments which needed to be made to build a team capable of developing systems like this and equip them with the right tools.

So the question being asked was: "why should we get distracted from our mainstream business which was paying our salaries, was nicely growing and making solid profits for company?"

Moreover, these kinds of projects were risky because of our inexperience—and if we failed to deliver satisfactorily, there was a danger of earning a bad name in the market.

"Why should we take that risk?"

Our argument was that this was a potentially much bigger opportunity. This was also a completely untapped market at that point in time. Not many Indian IT companies were doing anything in this area.

Moreover, many of our own customers—for whom we were building and maintaining all kinds of business applications—were spending a lot of money on research, development and engineering of their own products. Even if we made small inroads into their engineering departments, it could translate into rapid growth of our business.

In fact, the right time to pursue new directions of business is when the established business is running well and providing the company enough stability to take risks and explore uncharted territories.

There was still the question of whether our people had the capability and the knowledge of core engineering disciplines to execute these kind of projects.

As a matter of fact, we did—purely by chance!

As the IT industry, and along with it our own workforce, grew rapidly, the combined output of all universities could not have supplied the required number of people who were purely specialized in computer science and software engineering (in fact very few universities were actually teaching software engineering as a discipline).

Therefore we had been recruiting a large number of people with diverse engineering backgrounds, such as mechanical, electrical, chemical, electronics and communications and so on, and were making them learn software engineering (and, unlearn their core engineering knowledge in the process).

In order to successfully execute these "new" kind of projects we had the people with the right educational backgrounds. All we had to do was to stop forcing them to unlearn what they had learnt while earning their degrees and to convince them that practising what they had learned was also a viable career path for them.

They say, fortune favours the brave; that's exactly what happened.

We started talking to a large manufacturer of lifts based in Europe.

We all use lifts practically every day. All that we are concerned about is that when we press a button the lift should arrive quickly on the floor we are waiting at, and after pressing another button, it should stop on the floor where we desire to get off.

We are completely oblivious to the complexity of computations that need to happen behind the scene to make sure that your waiting time is minimized, you don't get trapped in between two floors, you reach the exact floor you desire to go and not somewhere else, the doors open and close long enough to let you enter and leave safely and all this is done efficiently enough to not waste your electricity.

In today's automated lifts all this is done by a controller unit which contains very sophisticated software. This controller software was the subject of discussion with this European lift-manufacturer.

They wanted to do a major technology upgrade of the controller of one of their very successful product lines. The technology originally used in the controller had started to become obsolete. Utilizing capabilities of newer electronics would have enabled them to provide new features in their product and keep it alive longer in the market. That meant that they also had to upgrade and reengineer the software that ran in the controller so that it could perform exactly the same tasks as the old controller—only faster. This is what they wanted us to do.

Ha, we thought, this was simple! All we had to do was make small changes and tweaks to the existing software wherever it was dependent on the specific characteristics of the old components in the old controller which were going to get replaced, to make it work with their newer replacements.

This is called "porting" in software engineering terms and while porting is not a trivial task, there exist well-established techniques to do it efficiently.

As we got deeper into planning the project, the genies in the bottle started popping out one by one.

Their first priority certainly was to get the old software ported to the newer controller to make it work exactly as the old controller did. However, in the process, they also wanted to make the ported software easily configurable so that adding any new features in the future would become significantly simpler.

That was a much tougher task because we had to build capabilities in the software apart from just "making it work", anticipating the needs of new features of the future and their engineering implications.

For example, one of the first new things they wanted to provide was a remote diagnostic capability i.e., in case some malfunction was reported in the operations of the lift, their maintenance engineers should be able to connect to the lift controller from their own office and examine the symptoms of the problem and, in simpler cases, even fix the problem remotely without having to visit the site where the lift was installed.

While successfully doing the work required to make the controller software work on the new controller platform, we also started learning all the intricacies and complex engineering which goes into making the lift a simple-to-use machine for the common user.

The single-biggest complaint from users of lifts is about the time they have to wait for the lift to arrive at the floor they are waiting at.

Where there are multiple lifts in the same building, such as an office complex, there is at least one obvious possibility of addressing this complaint. One could write an intelligent software program to optimize the waiting time by coordinating the movement of all the lifts. This is easier said than done. Such optimization problems are known to be some of the hardest problems to solve.

In this case at least you have multiple lifts to play with and, therefore, by taking into account where the various lifts are, which direction they are moving in, which buttons have been pressed by people in the lift etc., it is possible to determine which lift can get in the shortest-possible duration to the floor where you are waiting.

But what do you do when there is only one lift in a building? How do you minimize the waiting time?

You can increase the speed with which it moves but there are limits to how fast it can move. The faster it moves the more time it takes to come to a halt at the desired floor, so just hurtling the lift faster and faster does not help. Also, the faster it moves the more energy is wasted in bringing it to a halt.

Lifts also waste a lot of time when the doors of the lift are opening or closing.

Could you save that time by making the doors open and close faster and not leaving them open for too long? But in that case how do you avoid someone getting trapped between closing doors?

These are the kinds of problems that the lift-controller software (i.e., people like us who write that software) needs to anticipate and solve. These were the kind of innovations that our customer expected us to build in the lift-controller software.

Our customer also had many fancy ideas, which none of us had heard before. Many a time, generating innovative, mind-boggling ideas is the easy part. Finding ways of implementing them, in a practical, cost-effective and efficient manner is where the real challenges lie. And we were learning that fast.

They wanted to try out whether placing the floor buttons which are normally inside the lift could be placed outside the lift, i.e., you don't just have one button to press when you want a lift to come to where you are waiting, you also press the button for the floor to which you want to go.

This would increase the cost of installation because each floor will have to have a full keyboard installed instead of just one or two buttons. But the theory was that this would inform the controller in advance, the desired destination of each person waiting for a lift and would thus enable it to optimize the waiting time and the throughput (the total number of people transported in a given amount of time) of the lifts installed in a large building.

Could the opening and closing time of the doors of a lift be optimized by estimating how many people want to get into a lift at a particular floor or how many people wish to get out at a particular floor? Could the number of times the button to call the lift was pressed and the number of times a given floor button was pressed help in this estimation? Or could you install sensors outside the door to sense how many people are waiting?

In large, tall buildings and office complexes where thousands of people are moving up and down all the time, a great amount of space is wasted in the lift well—the duct in which the lift moves up and down because each such well contains only one lift. Could you actually then have multiple lifts in the same shaft moving independently of each other? How do you control and coordinate their movement so that they don't collide with each other by trying to go to the same floor at the same time?

Of course, all these ideas could be realized from a purely engineering point of view. But how much would it cost and would it really help in optimizing the waiting time and throughput so much that the extra cost would be worth it?

One couldn't answer such questions without actually building prototypes and trying out such outlandish ideas. So after finishing the core work we got engaged in constructing prototypes for several of these kind of ideas. Not all of those ideas, which were prototyped, actually got into the market immediately; some perhaps never did.

But, for us, this was exciting—we were building systems that had never been built before which, if successful, had the potential to make a positive impact on thousands of people who would use what we built! And we were getting paid handsomely for it. What more could we ask for.

For that matter, another positive result came out of it. Technologically perhaps not so exciting and intellectually perhaps not so challenging, it was something which helped put an end to the debate—whether it was worthwhile wasting our time on these new-fangled projects or whether it was better to stay focused on our mainstream IT business.

Lift as a product category, is a long-lived product. When a lift is installed once, it stays in use for decades. People don't replace lifts as casually they would change their cars. It is not unusual to see lifts in operation continuously for forty, fifty or more years and the users expect the manufacturer to maintain them through their lifetime.

Most of the maintenance concerns are mechanical wear and tear. However, if a product lives for this long, the technology in it also gets outdated and needs to be continuously enhanced to be current. And who better to maintain the technology than the people who developed it in the first place (for example, us in this case).

So we signed up a long-term contract with the customer to maintain the platform we had built for them and this work continues till today—more than a decade from the first time we started working on this project.

From a business point of view, this is a very valuable characteristic—predictability of future business for a long time to come.

That such longevity is possible even in this new-fangled business was the strongest argument we could present to end the debate and go full steam ahead in building a business in this new area.

The small team that I had started with my colleagues, Ajay and Ashwin, to explore this new area blossomed under Ajay's leadership into a vibrant and adventurous bunch. It went on to expand into full-fledged engineering of high-technology products for a diverse set of industries—from automotive to healthcare to consumer electronics and heavy-industrial equipment. The diversity of products and the requirements of our customers meant that every day we had a new challenge to face, every day a complex problem to solve. Moreover, the work we were doing was directly touching the lives of people who used these products and that had its own satisfaction.

The quality requirements of such systems were extremely high. Even the smallest mistake in the software could directly impact its users and could even cause fatal accidents—what if somebody is caught in the closing doors of a lift and the lift starts to move. If our software fails to detect this, it could mean risking somebody's life.

We worked with a Finnish company to re-engineer a crane which is used to load and unload containers to/from ships in a port. What if a small error in the software caused a container weighing several tons to drop on the deck of the ship from a height instead of being gently placed there?

What if a braking controller, which we were engaged in developing for a railway equipment manufacturer, failed to stop a train? The consequences would be catastrophic.

Our traditional customer base which consisted of banks and insurance companies and manufacturing companies also expected us to deliver error-free software for the business applications which we were building or maintaining for them. However, the cost of errors in such projects, at worst, would have been loss of business for us. In case of these engineering customers, our errors would put people's lives in danger. We were entering an area of mission-critical systems, which had no tolerance for errors of any kind.

That meant that we had to learn about and acquire very different quality control processes, tools and techniques. This also meant bringing about a cultural change in our people and teams—that finding a creative solution to an engineering problem is not the end of our responsibility, but making sure that, under all conceivable circumstances, the solution will work as expected is.

This is the most difficult challenge. New processes can be learned, tools and technology can be bought but imbibing an attitude of "no tolerance for errors" and maintaining that intolerance at the highest level is not easy.

CHAPTER FIFTEEN

Touching Lives

As I mentioned in the previous chapter, what was once considered a maverick idea was slowly accepted as a different road worth travelling on, because now every industry, from consumer goods to heavy industry to healthcare to automotive, was creating innovative products in its arena by including computing technology.

What has a rice cooker got to do with computer and software? One of the early projects we did for a Japanese customer consisted of writing software for a tiny computer (a micro-controller) which was to be embedded in a rice cooker to control its temperature and duration of cooking!

What has knee-replacement surgery got to do with computers and software? We were engaged to develop software to create a three-dimensional view of the knee joint of a patient using MRI scans. These 3D views were expected to help the surgeon plan how and where he would make the incision during the surgery to minimize damage to the healthy part of bones and tissues.

What has a rolling shutter, which is used to close the entrance to a shop or a garage, got to do with computers and software? We designed a fancy garage shutter control system using tiny micro-controllers. This shutter would sense the presence of the owner from a distance and open to welcome him just as his car reached the garage!

The opportunities for a company like ours were unlimited. The question was: how do we choose which areas/industries to pursue and not get distracted by all the exciting developments happening all around us.

Often, when successful people look back, it appears as if, in the past, right decisions were taken at the right time. However, I am not sure if, at the time those decisions are made, they are conscious choices with foresight. Often foresight is spotted only in hindsight!

Something similar happened to us.

The healthcare industry in general, and manufacturers of instruments, equipment and systems used in the healthcare industry in particular, innovate their products and technology at a furious pace. Adoption of computing technology in all aspects of their products accelerate continuously.

Healthcare is also an industry where the boom-and-bust cycles, which other manufacturers regularly suffer, are rare. For instance, see the ups and downs which the car manufacturers or the semi-conductor industry has seen periodically. As a supplier of services to the manufacturers, an industry that does not suffer from such unpredictability in their own markets is without question the ideal industry to focus on.

However, our forays in the healthcare industry started out purely by a fortuitous engagement with one such healthcare equipment manufacturer. The company's primary product was an artificial pacemaker.

We are all born with a natural system of regulating our heartbeat, depending on the circumstances we find ourselves in. For example, when we run, the heart needs to beat faster as compared to when we are, say, just walking or sleeping. This is done by cell structures called pacemaker nodes in the walls of our heart. The pacemaker nodes regulate the beating of the heart by stimulating the heart muscle with tiny electrical pulses.

Sometimes, for various reasons, these pacemaker nodes stop functioning as they should. This can be a life-threatening situation. A common remedy for this is to implant an artificial pacemaker which is a tiny electronic circuit which takes over the function of the natural pacemaker.

There are a number of challenges which a pacemaker manufacturer has to address. I am only mentioning those which concerned us—as an engineering and IT-solutions company.

Foremost, every pacemaker that is implanted in a patient has to be "programmed" to match that particular patient's needs and condition before it is surgically implanted. Even after it is implanted, from time to time, it needs to be reprogrammed because the patient's condition may demand some alteration in its functioning.

The cardiologists do this programming and re-programming using a device called a pacemaker programmer. The pacemaker programmer also functions as monitor to let the cardiologist review the condition of the patient's heart when the patient visits the cardiologist for periodic check-ups.

This pacemaker programmer is provided free of cost by the pacemaker manufacturer to the cardiologists. As the pacemaker technology improves the programmer also has to keep pace by upgrading itself. From the manufacturer's point of view this is a drain on its resources. They cannot recover the cost of the development of newer and newer programmers because they have to be offered free to the cardiologists.

For example, early pacemakers had to be connected to the programmer using wires. This meant that every time the need for re-programming arose, the patient had to undergo surgery. That had changed over a period of time and wireless pacemakers were developed which were capable of communicating with the programmer using radio waves.

However, to keep pace with this development the programmers had to be upgraded. They also had to be upgraded to make them more efficient, less costly to manufacture (since they were to be given free), more portable, etc.

All this meant substantial investment in R&D to keep pace with the pacemaker! Also, devices such as the pacemaker are highly regulated and need to meet stringent quality requirements laid down by the FDA (Food and Drug Administration agency of the US government).

The challenge thrown at us was: "Could you guys help us redesign the software running on the pacemaker programmer using modern technology in such a manner that the pacemaker programmer continues to function as it is? Also, in the process of this redesign, it should not violate or change any of the conditions under which FDA has certified this device for use."

We grabbed this opportunity with both hands and successfully developed the first version of this new programmer. During the course of this development, the real meaning of the word "quality" started to become starkly clear.

We were always a good, competent and conscientious company. We prided ourselves in never having lost a customer due to dissatisfaction with quality of our services.

But what was demanded in the pacemaker programmer project was a level of fanaticism for getting everything right the first time itself, which was unprecedented.

Literally, one bit not in its right place could make the difference between life and death for someone whose pacemaker was going to be programmed using the software we had built.

Building that first modernized version of the programmer wasn't the end of the story, however. Having fulfilled our customer's satisfaction, there was still a lot more in store for us.

Just creating a modern, more efficient, more portable programmer wasn't all that our customer was looking for. Given this modern platform, the idea was to create a series of products meant for everyday health monitoring for which someone might even be willing to pay! The idea was to convert what traditionally was a specialist's tool to a lifestyle device which the patient could use.

Those were the subsequent projects—some of which are continuing till date. One of the projects was to create a small device which a patient, with a pacemaker fitted in the body, could take home and keep it by bedside. This device could now keep the condition and functioning of the pacemaker continuously under surveillance. When the patient visited the cardiologist for periodic check-ups the data gathered by this bedside monitor would be very useful to the cardiologist.

Another improvement was to connect the bedside monitor to the internet and send the monitored data directly to the cardiologist. The idea was that the cardiologist would be in a position to review this data in advance and, in fact, be able to decide whether the patient needs to visit for a check-up at all!

When we started, this was, for us, purely an engineering problem—upgrading a product by replacing old technology with new. Something we had done many times in the past in different contexts. That is, exactly the kind of project where we had started working with the lift manufacturer.

In this case, it dawned on us pretty soon though, that good as our engineering skills may be, we need to learn a bit (actually quite a lot) about human physiology, the heart and its function in particular.

We were a bunch of engineers—learning about lifts and cranes, cars and trains and even digital music and rice cookers was not totally out of sync with what we had been trained to do.

Knowledge of human body and its constituent parts and their functions was a completely different realm that spoke a completely different language.

For a one-off project like this we just went to a couple of cardiologists who were personally known to some or the other in the team and got them to teach our team members at least the very basics.

As our business in the area of healthcare technology expanded into many different specialties within the medical profession, we had to create a formal support system consisting of doctors of different persuasion, diagnostics labs, hospitals etc., whose knowledge we could draw upon when a particular project required it.

The next important breakthrough that came our way was in the area of medical imaging. Medical imaging uses machines employing different techniques like X-Ray, CAT, MRI, PET, Ultrasound etc. for capturing images of human body.

These images are used by a specialist for diagnosing various kinds of ailments which a person may be suffering from. To look inside a particular part or organ of the body either you have to cut the body open or do chemical analysis of the externally accessible tissues and/or excretions from our body or use techniques like X-rays or ultrasound which enable you to view things hidden behind the skin and tissues.

The basic idea in all imaging technologies is to irradiate the required part of patient's body with radiation. X-rays and CAT scanners use electro-magnetic radiation of a particular range of frequencies. MRI uses a phenomenon called magnetic resonance. PET uses a beam of fundamental particles called positrons. Ultrasound scanning uses high-frequency sound (which our ears can't hear) etc.

Different types of tissues in our body absorb or reflect these different types of radiations quite differently. Therefore, each technique is useful to "see" only the type of tissue which strongly reflects the waves falling on it.

For instance, X-rays are useful to see bones but they pass right through softer organs in our body. In order to see, for example, areas of the brain in sufficient detail, you probably need to use an MRI scan. The extent of precise detail you can see is related to the wavelength of the radiation being used. The smaller the wavelength the greater the precision. However, as the wavelength becomes smaller, the energy content in it increases, and this increased amount of energy poses a threat to the healthy tissues that absorb it. So higher precision may carry a health risk. A balance has to be struck.

Second, the clarity of the picture is affected by many factors such as scattering of the waves by the tissues themselves or interference created by electrical or electronic equipment around the patient, etc. Therefore, the raw pictures obtained by any of these techniques are pretty much useless unless they are enhanced by utilizing various image-processing techniques which eliminate the noise and effects of scattering and interference.

Third, these pictures are flat two-dimensional (as any photograph usually is) with no sense of depth. The organs and tissues inside the patient's body, which a doctor is interested in examining, are three-dimensional structures. Therefore, for the doctor, it is important to be able to view them as they are.

A three-dimensional view of the organs can be constructed by taking several different images of the patient's body one after the other at different positions and then stitching them together.

This is almost like cutting a series of very thin slices of the human body, extracting information from each thin slice about the internal structure of the slice, and then stitching together each organ or tissue to construct the three-dimensional picture of that organ or tissue using the information extracted from the slices.

The doctors also like to view the organs from different directions. A photo usually provides a view only from one direction—the direction from which the photo was taken.

This is where computers and software come into play—to enhance the quality of the image, to construct a three-dimensional picture from multiple slices which have been recorded and to enable the doctor to view it from any direction by virtually rotating the constructed three-dimensional view as the doctor desires.

We started working with a major Japanese conglomerate, one of whose companies was a leading manufacturer of MRI and CAT scan systems.

The primary work we were engaged in consisted of developing different techniques and improving existing software for image enhancement and three-dimensional rendition of the captured images.

In addition to simply developing techniques to create better and clearer images, we also started working on techniques to identify features in the image that were of interest to the doctor who would be looking at them. So, instead of just providing a clearer picture, the system would also identify and highlight structures of potentially special interest.

The basic techniques of image processing can be utilized for a wide variety of medical diagnostic applications—besides being used in machines like X-ray, CAT/MRI/PET or ultrasound.

For example, while the work for this Japanese company was going on, a very different kind of problem was presented to us by an American company.

The objective was to create a system that can be used to provide medical assistance to a patient located in a remote location where it is impossible for a doctor to reach the patient in person.

The first such situation which they wanted to tackle was when a person on a ship on the high seas needs to be examined by a specialist medical professional located on land somewhere far away. Apart from the distance and inability to reach quickly where the patient is, the major constraint in this situation is the limited availability of telecommunications facilities.

Of course, ship-to-shore communication, using satellite telephony, had advanced significantly compared to the days when the only means of communicating with someone on the shore was limited to Morse coded messages (like the telegraph).

Still, the capacity of these systems would be severely stretched if full motion real-time video contact needed to be established between the patient on the ship and the doctor on the shore for the doctor to visually examine the patient. This was the challenge we had to overcome.

Usual techniques of video compression to fit the video within the constraints of the ship's communication system also reduce the quality and clarity of the video severely making it almost unusable for medical diagnostic purposes.

We had to evolve software which could cleverly identify the portions of each video frame which were not of any interest to the doctor and transmit them with very-low quality. For example, if the doctor is examining the bleeding nose of a person, he does not need to be able to see the whole face of the person with equal clarity.

The doctor could direct the video camera to focus on some particular feature or part. This would be recognized by the software automatically and only that part would be transmitted with good quality and the remaining objects in the visual field of the camera would be severely compressed.

This is relatively easy to do for a still photograph. When a video stream is being transmitted in real time, the focus of the camera keeps shifting continuously. The software has to continuously identify what part of the current frame is to be compressed by compromising quality and which part to be left alone to provide good visibility to the doctor.

This project was a resounding success and the basic techniques we developed then got applied to create systems for many different situations.

We started using image-processing technology in yet another area. This is the field of digital pathology. Usually in a pathology lab, small, thin slices of tissues or samples of blood or saliva and so on are stained using various chemical processes, placed in a glass slide and examined under the microscope by the pathologist.

This microscopic examination can be greatly enhanced by using image-processing techniques. An image processing technique called feature extraction can be very effectively used to provide assistance to the pathologist. The applications of such techniques in the pathology labs are wide ranging; from identifying infectious pathogens to diagnosis of cancer.

As I mentioned, the image-processing technology can be used for a wide-ranging medical applications; not just diagnosis of ailments by providing greater visibility to the doctors but also for therapeutic procedures such as surgeries.

We got involved in a very interesting project. The subject was neurosurgery. Surgical procedures performed on the brain are some of the most delicate and potentially hazardous operations which require great precision and care.

One such procedure called deep brain stimulation requires a probe to be inserted in the affected part of the brain. Inserting the probe by drilling a hole in the skull and pushing the probe to exactly the desired location of the brain without damaging healthy cells in the brain is a very delicate task.

In order to aid a surgeon planning to perform such a surgery, we were required to write software which would construct a three-dimensional map of the brain from several MRI scans. This map would then be used to plan the exact path through which the probe could be inserted in the brain by causing minimal damage to the healthy tissues in the way.

During the actual surgery the software would continuously show, on a monitor, the planned path and the actual movement of the probe as it is being inserted so that the surgeon (who couldn't otherwise see what was happening inside the skull) would be able to ensure he was following the carefully planned path.

This was exacting work. Even the smallest of errors in our software had the potential to cause irreparable harm to the patient. The project was eminently successful and lead to more work to adopt the same technology for a very different kind of surgical procedure—that of knee-replacement surgery.

Now, knee replacement can be considered not as delicate and hazardous a procedure as an operation of the brain. However, any surgery is potentially dangerous. The concept in this project was the same—use a series of MRI images to create a three-dimensional map of the internal bone structures of the patient's knee and utilize this map to carry out the surgery with minimal damage to healthy bones.

The widespread usage of computing technology in medical equipment meant we had to create specialist laboratories within our company to house a diverse set of medical devices. Our laboratories which occupy one whole floor in our office probably contain as much (if not more) medical hardware as a small hospital! This also often lands us in strange situations.

We needed to install an ultrasound (sonography) machine in our lab to work on a project for one of our customers.

Ever since people discovered that ultrasound machines could be used to determine the gender of the unborn child, they have been widely abused by using the results for infanticide. As a result the government strictly regulates their use to ensure they are not used for gender determination.

When we asked for the government's permission to install an ultrasound machine, there was a great deal of suspicion about our motives.

"Why do you, an IT company, need an ultrasound machine? Surely you are cooking up some Machiavellian scheme to misuse it" was the first reaction.

We had to spend a lot of time and effort to convince the authorities that we had no evil intentions. All that we wanted the machine for was to test the software we were going to write to improve the quality of its image processing.

A similar obstacle arose when we needed to install a mammography machine. Mammography machines emit high dosage of X-rays which could be potentially harmful if a person is exposed to them for a long period of time. We had to first construct a properly shielded room, get it certified from an authorized agency and only then were allowed to import and install the machine.

Such unexpected obstacles apart, employing computing technology in the field of medicine was an eminently satisfying proposition. It was not only "just good business" but it was gratifying to think that doing our job right was making a difference to someone in improving the quality of their lives!

CHAPTER SIXTEEN

A New Chapter but the Same Story
2011

In 1983, I had gotten engulfed in the maelstrom of information technology. And, nearly thirty years later, I was still hypnotized by the wonders writ all around me by this phenomenon called computer.

As a teenager, I had spent sleepless nights, awe-struck, reading about science-fiction tales of the super computer Multivac and "positronic" robots conjured up by Isaac Asimov. As an adult, I was spending sleepless nights bringing into reality Asimov's flights of fancy.

The pursuit of exploring the limits of what computers can do had taken me to far corners of the world. I was spending more time in the seat of an airplane than on the ground.

Once in a while, I would find myself ensconced in the warmth of home and I would ask myself, "How long?"

This was not a case of getting jaded or falling into a rut of the same routine. Not at all.

A whole new arena of applications driven by the all-pervasive Internet was emerging and disrupting established products and services. Amazon was the "place" people were going shopping, not Walmart or Sears. Kindle was where people were buying books, not Barnes and Noble. You didn't stand on the street corner on 5th Avenue in Manhattan, braving snow and whistle for a taxi. You sat in the warmth of your hotel room, tapped on your mobile phone and a taxi would zoom in at your doorstep.

Even enterprises did not need to "buy" computers anymore. They could purchase "computing power" by the hour! If anything, new things were happening and providing opportunity to be creative at a pace faster than before.

There were two unrelated factors driving me to ask the question, "How long did I want to stay enmeshed in this, with wheels on my feet, living a schedule dictated by the demands of my customers?"

First, fascinating as my professional world was, there was a whole different universe out there for which I had little or no time. Second, things were starting to take a turn in an unexpected, uncomfortable and disturbing direction within Patni.

By any yardstick, my professional journey was without any significant bumps and obstacles until that point in time. This was partly because I happened to be present at the right time, in the right place, armed with the right education in a field that was just taking off to conquer the world. Partly, this also was because I was genuinely in love with what I was required to do and had the ability to do it well.

From the first serious project in my B.Tech. days that sought to apply computing technology to monitor cardiac patients, to the latest project consisting of developing the next-generation MRI technology, in a sense, I had come a full circle.

A lot had changed during this thirty-year circle. Computers, which were an unapproachable entity, ensconced in a glass-walled temple, had become the hidden prime mover behind every industrial and nearly every consumer activity, and in my own small way I had contributed to this transformation.

There was a different dimension to this transformation that had taken place closer to home.

Thirty years ago India as a country was a complete non-entity in the global industrial landscape. We produced nothing that anybody in the outside world wanted or valued, we were known for nothing which the industrial world outside India respected. Our most notable exports then were Pt Ravishankar and Bhagwan Rajneesh! People from outside came to India seeking spiritual gurus, not engineering excellence.

All of this had changed when Indian IT industry challenged and beat the then giants of IT industry in the world, at their own game, in their own backyard.

To be sure, IT industry was not the only segment of Indian enterprises which conquered the world during this time. An Englishman sipping Tetley tea (owned by Tatas) at breakfast in his home and driving on the M-5 to work in a Jaguar (also owned by Tatas) was a sure sign that the "Raj" was well and truly over and India had something to offer that the world coveted besides Yoga.

However we, the IT Industry, were unquestionably the path breakers.

There were, however, ominous signs that the wave which the Indian IT industry had ridden successfully for two decades or more was gradually dissipating as every wave must, someday. That does not mean they were performing badly or losing customers and markets or were going bankrupt—far from it. Clearly, their business model had lost its sheen and was becoming commoditized.

What do I mean by "commoditized"? When it becomes easy for a competitor to emulate you, when your buyers buy your product purely based on its cost and not value, when your prospective customers start asking you to talk to the "vendor manager" and not to the "business leader", when the only way in which you can win new business is by having to participate in a formal tender/bid process—you can be sure that your business model has become commoditized.

In such a situation either you learn to live with ever-increasing pressure on your pricing and profit margins and change your organization into a lean, mean outfit that can walk on the edge of a razor or try and reinvent your value proposition to get out of this trap of commoditization. Almost everybody in the IT industry had seen this headwind becoming stronger and stronger over the last few years and were taking measures to counter it in different ways.

These were challenging times for any organization, but for us, in Patni, this was an especially tricky situation. Patni was and remained a family-owned and run company—notwithstanding its having gone public and its shares getting listed on stock exchanges in India and the US.

It was founded by the three brothers—Gajendra, Narendra and Ashok Patni—and ever since had been run by them. However, it was becoming clear that the unanimity of purpose that was present once amongst the founders, for whatever reasons, no longer existed. There were definite indications that at least some of the founders wanted to sell their stake in the company off and exit. Given the large stake they held, it was also clear that if they were to sell it, a change of control of the company was inevitable.

The word of this possibility had reached some of our customers. Several of them, where we had become over a period of time a critical part of their own IT strategy, were becoming jittery and we were already getting caught in fending off their queries about it.

The gradual dilution of the value of our services due to the commoditization and this uncertainty about the future of our company was a lethal combination. The company needed to reinvent itself, but the uncertainty at the top-most level meant who and how this transformation will be driven wasn't clear.

I was almost getting ready to chuck it all. I was already in my late fifties, in a fortunate position to not have to worry about getting a monthly pay cheque, with wide interests which would keep me occupied and yet not require a big fortune to support.

Just about then the inevitable happened. IGATE, a company about one-third the size of Patni bought out the Patni founders and gained control of the company. There was a brief interlude before that when the founders brought in a new CEO in place of Naren Patni who had led the organization from its inception. However, that had not resulted in addressing any of the uncertainties that Patni was struggling to cope with.

Change of control for any organization is a turbulent time. For any person it takes a while to understand fully the implications of such a change. Things you have become used to, things which you take for granted and assumptions on the basis of which you plan your professional life suddenly become invalid and non-existent. Your notions of expected and accepted behaviour, your formulas for personal success, are no longer guaranteed. And the uncertainty around all this is the greatest for those who are at the top of the heap.

For those of us who had worked closely with the Patnis for nearly three decades in building this company up from a couple of hundred people to a 16,000-people strong family, this was an especially trying time.

Would I be treated with the same respect that I had earned through hard work over three decades in Patni? Would I even be "wanted" by the new owners? Even if the answers to both of these questions were positive, had my arteries hardened so much that I would find it impossible to adapt to the new environment? Did I even want to try to find answers to these questions? I wasn't sure.

Then it occurred to me that perhaps these kinds of demons are more in my mind and the uncertainty more fearsome in my imagination than in reality. I realized that I was getting ready to chuck it all a little while ago anyway and that route was always going to remain open. So there seemed no reason to not wait and actually see what the future had in store. If I did not get along with a new bunch of colleagues, no one could stop me from walking away!

IGATE buying Patni was big news—this was the largest transaction of this kind that happened till that time (of course, Tech Mahindra had bought over Satyam before that but that had happened under very different and sort of unsavoury circumstances so that is really not a fair comparison). As is their wont—reporters were publishing stories in newspapers which had some grain of truth but were generously garnished with hearsay. For myself and people like me with long years of association with Patni it was difficult to not read them with considerable anguish.

Personally, this takeover actually brought about a refreshing change.

About eight to ten years ago, I had fought hard to implement this whole idea of undertaking true engineering projects and R&D services (as opposed to our bread-and-butter IT-services business). After helping to establish the foundations for a sustainable business out of it, I had moved away from it to take up other responsibilities in Patni.

When IGATE took over Patni, Ajay Chamania, under whose leadership this business had blossomed, in the interim, decided to leave and pursue his own interests. I was, therefore, asked to step in and once again take charge of what in any case was close to my heart. Whether right or wrong, in my eyes the kind of work we were doing in this area was always the "true" purpose of computing technology. This, therefore, was a welcome change!

New identity card, new logo, new PowerPoint template for preparing presentations to be given to customers, new colours on the office building, occasional clashes with a new culture and a new CEO to report to. It was almost like starting a new school year. The only thing missing was perhaps the smell of new books and a new uniform!

But I had no time to think of or to worry about the change.

I had come back to the engineering and R&D services area after a gap of many years. While as a senior officer of Patni I was generally aware of what was going on in that part of the business, I had been hands-off it for a long time.

A lot had happened in the interim; new customers, new creative ideas that had been implemented, new segments of the industry that had been penetrated. There was a lot to catch up on. Especially important was establishing relationships with the customers who we were serving and prospects which we were chasing at the time this change took over. More than ever I was finding myself belted into an airplane seat—so much so that I had started recognizing the flight crew members on board.

But all that was well worth it, from one point of view.

I was learning about completely new, creative applications of computing technology, even in segments of the industry that have been—perhaps unfairly—called "Smoke Stack" industry, usually pictured as housed in ugly red-brick sheds with dirty corrugated roofs, tall funnels belching out clouds of thick black smoke, burly men in dirty coveralls with rusty shovels pushing heaps of coal into the gaping red mouth of a sooty furnace.

Undoubtedly, that is how the railroads and associated industries—like the manufacturers of railway engines or freight cars—were some decades ago. However, the manufacturer of railway braking systems from Germany that we had started working with just before IGATE took over Patni, had moved on to be a high-tech company a very long time ago.

What do the brakes of a train have to do with computers? Applying brakes to stop any moving vehicle is the simplest of acts one can imagine, right?

When you press the brake lever on your bicycle, all that happens is that a cube of rubber gets pressed against the rim of the moving wheel and the friction causes the wheel to slow down and stop. The cube of rubber needs to be replaced once in a while because it wears off and the faster you are moving the harder you have to press the piece of rubber but that is about all the intelligence required to apply the brakes.

Sure, if the vehicle is heavier and can move faster than a bicycle, you would need a mechanism to create a greater frictional force and perhaps a simple piece of rubber won't be adequate, you might need a piece of some other tougher material.

A train is perhaps the heaviest vehicle on land and therefore much greater force will be needed to make it stop and perhaps some very tough material to act as the braking "rubber" but what role could a computer conceivably play and justify its presence in a braking system?

Well, imagine what will happen if a train moving at 100 or 150 kmph is to be stopped and the brakes are only mounted on the wheels of the engine pulling the train. If it were a bicycle, it would be quite simple. Even if you pressed the brake lever of *only* the front wheel, the rear wheel would also stop, and vice versa.

But, what will happen when the brakes slow down *only* the engine of the train? According to Isaac Newton (whom we met in high-school physics class) the rest of the train will want to continue to travel with the speed at which it was travelling and crush the engine because of its enormously greater momentum.

So in the first place, braking a train successfully will need a braking system on every car connected to the train. Moreover, the application of brakes of all cars, needs to be synchronized extremely precisely. So that every car slows exactly at the same rate—even one car falling out of step even by the smallest amount will cause the train to derail! Remember a long freight train may be pulling even fifty or more freight-laden cars.

It is totally unrealistic to expect that the brake pads that actually rub against the wheels to create friction are worn out by exactly the same amount on all the cars in a train. What if on some cars the brake pads are worn more than others or what if they are more worn on the left wheels than on the right? How do you ensure that the braking will still be in perfect synchronization? And given the huge momentum of a moving train, how do we ensure that even though the wheels stop rotating successfully, they won't skid on the rails?

Suddenly the problem of braking a train has become orders of magnitude more complex than simply applying the required amount of force depending on the weight and speed of the moving train. The sophistication in the engineering of train-braking systems and the intelligence required to be built in the braking-control units has been much farther ahead of the braking systems in cars or other vehicles.

For example, anti-lock braking technology was developed by train manufacturers decades before automobile manufacturers caught on. That is why technology—the best that is available at any given time—has always been utilized in railway-braking systems. However, technology changes practically every day and integrating better and better technology as it becomes available becomes a continuous effort. That was exactly what we were engaged to do for this German company.

While this engagement was getting established, something even more exciting came along. We were chosen to set up an innovation centre by one of the world's largest mining company.

Mining? Isn't that where you blast holes into a mountain side, teams of tough guys with pick-axes and shovels go down those holes and come back pushing wheel barrows laden with rocks and dirt and coal which they have dug out of those holes? Well, I wasn't quite as naïve as all that but when we first started talking to this mining company my mental picture of a mining operation was not particularly high-tech.

In fact, the whole idea behind setting up the innovation centre was that we didn't know anything about mining! The expectation was that because we were ignorant about mining we would approach the problems our customer wanted solved without any preconceived ideas and would come up with out-of-the-box solutions. In reality that wasn't quite the case. We had to have at least some rudimentary appreciation of the mining business if we were to come up with effective solutions.

As we started understanding more and more about their operations, the picture emerging was quite mind blowing. First to hit me was the scale of everything—gigantic. Even the tyre of a truck that hauls ore from the mines was twice as tall as a human being. Just changing the tyre on such a truck was an operation that kept the truck out of circulation for many days. The second thing that struck me was just how hazardous the lives are of those who work in the mines. A smallest miscalculation or a tiniest error in judgement, could mean a disastrous accident endangering the lives of people. Workplace safety was therefore an extremely serious matter.

Several of the projects we did for the mining company in due course of time represented large investments in technology in the hope that it could improve safety at the workplace.

For example, in one of the early projects, we were presented with the problem of finding a way to detect the presence of a person in a ship's cargo hold.

In many of their mines the ore taken out from the mine is loaded on a ship anchored at a nearby port (they own and operate their own ports). People need to go inside the hold to clean or to do other maintenance activities. Therefore, before the cranes on the port can start dumping the ore in the cargo hold, someone has to go in physically and check if any workers are still inside.

The fear was—due to a slip up of some sort—either somebody forgets to go and check, or even if someone checks, the holds are so big that an inspector may easily miss a solitary worker. If something like that happens the worker inside could die under the tons of ore that gets dumped in the hold. So an automated system was sought to be designed that would detect if the hold was empty and only after it was found empty the crane would be able to operate.

This sounds like not such a difficult problem to crack—just insert a camera in the hold, scan the hold by rotating the camera in a full circle, transmit the pictures taken to a video monitor up in the harbour and the crane operator can see whether the hold was empty or not.

That is what we thought when we first heard of this problem. However, in the first place, normal cameras couldn't be guaranteed to work and produce usable pictures of the inside of the hold. This meant that we had to find a different technique to capture the images of the inside of a hold that will be more reliable than normal cameras.

Second, they did not want to rely on any manual intervention at all. This implied that we had to develop image-processing techniques to analyse the pictures and automatically detect whether the image contained a human being.

We experimented and concluded that a thermal camera stood the best chance of being able to provide the required reliability. Remember the technique needed to be 100 per cent foolproof—where safety of a person was concerned there were no compromises!

A thermal camera is sensitive to infrared radiation, i.e., heat emissions and thus detects temperature variations, just as a normal camera which is sensitive to visible light detects variations in illumination. The idea was that if there was a person present in the hold, the temperature of his body would create a temperature variation pattern distinctly different from that of an empty hold.

This was easier said than done, however. None of my team members had ever been on a cargo ship and none had ever seen what a ship's cargo hold looks like from the inside.

The environment inside is never stable. First, the ship is bobbing on the water even when it is anchored and stationary in the port. So the whole hold is constantly moving randomly up and down. Second, the temperature pattern inside is never stable. As the day progresses and the sun shines on the ship and its hold the temperature inside varies. A small puddle of water inside creates a very localized temperature variation pattern that on a thermal image could very well be misinterpreted as the presence of a person and so on.

Unless you have seen it, it is difficult to imagine just how hard it would be to develop a technique to analyse the thermal images to detect with 100 per cent certainty that the hold was empty.

The first few attempts failed miserably to achieve the required level of reliability. Finally, we had to create a scaled-down model of a hold, first in our labs to study what a hold may look like inside. We would artificially create different patterns of temperature variation and test our techniques against it.

That was a long and tedious task and I must spare you the details. All I can say is that only after much hard work we were able to fine tune our methods to reach the required accuracy and the project was successfully completed.

*****

The innovation programmes in this centre were not, of course, confined only to developing safety systems. However, foolproof safety had to be a no-compromise attribute of every system that we developed eventually.

The possibilities for being creative in all the different areas of a mine operation were endless. The operations of a mining business can be broadly classified into four areas—

1. *Exploration* This requires surveying a wide geographical area to locate exactly where the minerals of interest may be buried under the earth.
2. *Excavation* Having located the deposits of the minerals of interest, dig into the earth and bring the rocks and dirt containing the minerals out of the mine.
3. *Transportation* Move the rocks and dirt from the mine site to the processing factories where the minerals will be extracted.

Just how large are these transportation operations? Our customer was the largest owner of private railway tracks in the whole country—larger even than the national railways!

4. *Processing* It is the actual extraction of the minerals from the rocks and dirt.

We wound up eventually working on systems in many of these areas.

For example, one of the projects that we started working on was aimed at creating an intelligent vehicle that could work without active supervision of a human operator and plant explosives for blasting open large tracts of land for mining.

Planting explosives is both a very complex and hazardous operation. The explosives have to be planted in small holes drilled into the ground at just the right places, in just the right amount over acres of land—land which is essentially wild and untamed.

First, the area is surveyed and the maps produced in the survey are analysed to determine where exactly the holes have to be drilled and how much explosive is to be placed in each hole.

Then someone has to drive a special vehicle like a truck over this area. The truck carries the explosives and drills are mounted on the truck. The truck goes and stops over a pre-determined location, the driver operates the drill and digs a hole of just the right depth, deposits a pre-determined amount of explosive in it and moves on to the next location.

The system we were designing was aimed at automating all of these activities. Most importantly the truck had to be driverless! Capable of moving on its own, being able to determine all the obstructions in its way like ditches, large rocks, slopes and valleys, small hills, water bodies, marshy patches and finding its way to the pre-determined locations. It had to be capable of sensing the nature of the soil at the drill location and thus determining exactly how to drill the hole and exactly how much explosive to deposit in it.

Creating all that intelligence in a truck was not easy. So initially a remote-controlled version of the truck was to be created where the driver will sit in the control room, he will be able to see whatever the truck was "observing" through its cameras and direct the truck using a remote control.

In the second step, the remote control was to be eliminated altogether. It is not easy to create a fully autonomous, driverless vehicle capable of moving around on a flat predictable surface. A vehicle capable of negotiating wild unpredictable terrain was orders of magnitude more difficult.

I could go on and on about these kinds of flights of fancy which we were attempting to bring to reality.

Another project consisted of using GPS technology for an unusual purpose. The most common use of GPS technology is in car-navigation systems. The GPS satellites help pin point our location on the ground and using the location and a map stored in your smart phone, you can navigate your way through the labyrinth of any modern city.

GPS satellites, however, also help us pin point our elevation from the mean sea level—this is of little use in a car-navigation system. But this was the capability that we were going to use to determine how empty or full a ship's cargo holds might be and thus enabling automated cranes in the harbour to decide how much ore to load in the hold! The idea was to use GPS technology to determine how high the ship is riding on the water—and empty ship would be riding higher and a ship loaded with ore would settle lower in the water.

Again, the idea is deceptively simple, its realization in an automated system devilishly difficult.

Even an anchored ship isn't quite stationary like a standing car. It keeps bobbing up and down and tilts this side and that and pitches forwards and backwards randomly all the time. All of these movements keep changing the GPS readings all the time—so you have to develop techniques to cancel out this random movement and then determine how high the ship is riding on the water.

These kinds of developments aren't short-term efforts. Often solutions that seem feasible turn out to be useless when they are field tested. There are so many variables in the environment in which the solution has to work that it is impossible to account for them while you are designing the system in an air-conditioned lab! One has to go back to the drawing board and start all over again.

I would have loved to see these great ideas being fully realized and operational in the real world.

However, by then I had found the answer to the question I was asking myself just before IGATE took over Patni.

I had had a great run in Patni. Despite the turmoil of the takeover, I had found my moorings in the new set-up after the takeover and had contributed significantly enough to be given the CEO's award—for the stellar performance my team had delivered in the first year itself after the takeover.

I had seen the world change in three decades (and as I would like to believe) more profoundly than ever before because of (and again as I would like to believe) the most important invention of all time—that of the computer. And in my small way I had contributed to this change.

It was time to do something else. I didn't know precisely what else but 5th of December of 2013 was approaching, which was my birthday, and it looked like a good idea to hang up my laptop on that day. As it happened things got stretched a bit till middle of the following year before I could really do so but that was just a minor blip.

CHAPTER SEVENTEEN

A Welcome Invasion

Throughout history, advances in science and technology have always impacted human lives in a dramatic manner and, more often than not, for the better. Whether it is the invention of the wheel or Galileo's telescope or the steam engine or the telephone or the television, they have enabled us to extend capabilities of our sensory and motor systems beyond the limits imposed by our bodies.

Telescopes have allowed us to see things so far away which our naked eye can never see. Cars have enabled us to travel faster than our bare feet can ever run. Airplanes have made it possible for us to fly which our bodies aren't built to do. Cranes have enabled us to lift weights far greater than our own hands can ever lift. Telephones help us talk with people at distances our voice can never span.

Long before practically usable computers were created, long before they became ubiquitous enough to enter our day-to-day lives visibly or invisibly, science-fiction writers had dreamt of their existence. Science-fiction writings of the 1940s, '50s and '60s contain fanciful accounts of "intelligent" computing machines in every form and shape that you can imagine.

Broadly, these "intelligent" computing machines in those stories fell into two categories. As Isaac Asimov has called them, robots-as-a-menace and robots-as-a-pathos stories. The first category contained stories of machines that—having gone berserk—were bent on destroying their creator. Most of these stories were essentially technological versions of the story of the Garden of Eden and the Original Sin—the sin of consuming from the tree of knowledge of good and bad. They were meant to teach a moral lesson to their readers. The second category contained stories of essentially "intelligent" and lovable pets or servants abused and ill-treated by cruel human beings. Asimov was probably the first to popularize stories that treated robots and other intelligent computing machines as an industrial product, designed and built by level-headed engineers for a practical and useful application.

That is what all machines are—an industrial product, designed and built by level—headed engineers for a practical and useful application. They are not designed and built to compete with human capabilities, they are built to enhance them.

That is why we didn't see a Ferrari or a Porsche announcing a contest between their fastest car and Carl Lewis (when he was the fastest man on earth). Nor did we see a speed-boat manufacturer boasting in an advertisement that their speed-boat will outpace Mark Spitz—the winner of seven Olympic golds and simultaneous world record holder in all seven events! Even when clearly the slowest Ferrari and the slowest speed-boat were several times faster than Lewis and Spitz respectively, neither Lewis and Spitz or their fellow athletes nor lay people at large ever felt "threatened" by this superiority.

All through the history of technological triumphs one human faculty—our mind and intellect—has remained uniquely human and beyond the purview of the mightiest of the machines. The evolution of computers has, however, been encroaching slowly but surely into this unique human preserve. This is not to say that computers have today or ever will surpass and replace the human mind. However, they are surely starting to do to our intellectual faculties what other products of technology did to our physical capabilities, i.e., extending the power of our minds into realms that our bare minds would be hard put to reach, on their own.

But if the development of computers is nothing more than the development of a tool to enhance our (intellectual) capabilities, why did we then see in 1997 a "grudge" rematch being announced between Deep Blue, IBM's chess-playing computer, and Gary Kasparov? Billed as an opportunity for Deep Blue to get even with the world chess champion for the loss that it had suffered in 1996. Why did Shakuntala Devi find it necessary to advertise her show with a claim that she was "faster than any computer"? Clearly, there seems to be an undercurrent of competition or resentment over this encroachment by the modern-day computers into areas that we believe are the essence of our "humanness".

If you recall, right in the introduction of this book, I had asked: "All our lives, what have all of us been conditioned to believe, are the visible indicators of intelligence?" Hopefully the examples through subsequent pages of this book have provided sufficient illustration of the fact that on every one of those "conventional" indicators, today's computers perform better than any human being that has ever lived on this earth.

That does not mean computers have become more intelligent than us but that does mean that the very definition (and along with that the common perception) of "intelligence" or more broadly "humanness" needs to be reexamined and revised.

That is precisely why when Deep Blue did get even by beating Kasparov in the rematch in 1997, there raged a spectacular debate in the academia as well as among lay people whether this means that computers can really be considered "intelligent".

This debate is actually meaningless, though; unless you are able to define unambiguously what the debate is about, i.e., what is the definition of "intelligence"?

Alan Turing did come up with one such definition. Let me attempt a simplified description just to convey the concept. Turing's actual description is different and more complex. Turing defined an experiment. Suppose you are sitting in front of a small window in a wall. The window is so small that you cannot see what is on the other side but you can exchange small chits of paper on which you can write anything you want. There is some thing on the other side which responds to whatever you write by typing on another chit which gets pushed through the window to you. If after spending sufficiently long time (as long as you wish) you are not able to decide whether whoever is responding to your chits is another human being or a computer, based purely on the interaction that you have been engaged in, then whatever is on the other side should be considered as intelligent.

This proposal called the "Turing Test" has been opposed on many grounds. The most important opposition stems from the fact that there is no requirement of "understanding", "knowledge", "thought", "consciousness" or notions like that in the Turing Test. And Intelligence cannot exist without understanding anything, without feeling anything, without even being "alive".

This objection is troublesome because it invokes in support of itself several other notions which in turn are not clearly defined—thought, consciousness, etc. One could argue that if a machine's behaviour is indistinguishable from that of a human being, what makes you believe that the machine just by being built out of metal, plastics and semi-conductors doesn't actually "feel" what the human being is feeling?

Modern-day computers aren't yet quite capable of passing the Turing Test. However, they aren't too far from being able to do so.

There is yet another and probably a more practical (and less emotional, compared to the earlier) objection to the Turing Test. This concerns Turing Test's basic presumption that intelligence is defined by whatever a human being does. The question that is being asked is—Why is human behaviour the only yardstick of intelligent behaviour?

For example, we don't define "flying" by saying "flying" is whatever a bird does. We, in fact, did do so a century ago and tried to achieve the ability to fly by emulating the behaviour of birds. Adventurous young men built wings covered with feathers and jumped off buildings wildly flapping them like they had seen the birds do. They all plunged to their doom.

It is only when science had advanced enough to understand the meaning of "flying" independent of the method used by birds, that the Wright Brothers were able to produce a flying machine—that did not flap its wings, which did not need any feathers but which undoubtedly flew and did so far better than any bird on earth has ever managed to do.

Intelligence should be understood in the same way first, say the proponents of this objection to the Turing Test, and we should not get our definition cluttered and confused with the method human beings may be using to achieve and display it. Perhaps like the airplanes, computers don't need to flap their mental wings to be intelligent.

Regardless of this debate and regardless of who may be right and who may be wrong in this debate, one fact remains. No machine, before computers came along, has questioned some of our very basic assumptions about what makes us, well, humans!

The foremost question is—why is that? Why is the impact of computers on our lives so pervasive? Why do computers have the potential to affect (mostly positively) in almost endless ways, practically every facet of our lives? This is unlike every other machine invented in the past, each of which impacted only a very focused, narrow sliver of our lives.

All along through the school I had been taught (as are all of us) that "computing" meant manipulating "numbers"—you add them, you multiply them, divide them or subtract them. Even when I later learned more complicated mathematics of complex numbers and integral calculus, and so on, it was still all to do with numbers. Complex numbers are strange and behave in unintuitive ways but they are still numbers. Integration and differentiation are much more complicated operations as compared to addition or subtraction but they still manipulate numbers.

The first time that I had an inkling that perhaps this was a very narrow and restrictive view of computation, without necessarily fully understanding why, was when I read about George Boole and his book *The Laws of Thought*.

Logical reasoning as I understood it until that point in time was a quintessentially human ability driven by something undefinable and unfathomable called our mind. And here was George Boole presenting a precise mathematical formulation of that ability. This formulation or system—Boolean algebra—provides the fundamental underpinning of all computers. One could therefore argue that computers are "logical" machines performing acts of logical reasoning (without needing to "understand" the meaning of the words either "logic" or "reasoning")!

This was an intriguing conclusion—a machine built to operate according to the rules of this system could perform an activity that has always been considered the very hallmark of an intelligent being. While that thought was unconsciously germinating in my mind, I was learning, as if on a parallel track, how to program computers, how they are designed and built, what intricate electronic circuitry powers them. It slowly started becoming apparent that "computing" represents something much wider than the meaning one would colloquially associate with it.

Boole's algebra contains no numbers! The elements of this system have no meaning. We could decide that the elements mean "a switch is ON" and "a switch is OFF" and then use the rules of this system to represent an electrical switching circuit. Or we could decide that the elements stand for "TRUE" and "FALSE" and use the system to represent a logical argument (such as the proof you may write to prove Pythagoras's theorem). Or we could decide that they stand for the numbers 1 and 0 and then use the rules to represent arithmetic operations on numbers (such as adding numbers, subtracting numbers, multiplying numbers, and so on). Therefore, if we decided to define "computing" to mean whatever it is that "computers" do then clearly "computing" ought to mean doing many more things in addition to manipulating numbers!

That is where Alan Turing entered my life. Alan Turing defined a very simple hypothetical device. The device essentially manipulates "symbols"—it can "read" symbols written on a tape—one at a time. Write a new symbol on the tape or replace an already written symbol on the tape according to a set of rules (when to read, when to replace and when to write and when to do nothing but move to the next symbol). The symbols have no meaning, nor do the rules necessarily mean anything. It is precisely because this system is inherently "meaningless", it is so powerful.

By defining an appropriate set of rules (i.e., by "programming" Turing's device) and assigning an appropriate "meaning" to the symbols, one can make Turing's machines perform (in principle) practically any task which can be specified in a "finite" number of steps—whether it is performing numerical calculations, whether it is deciding if a given sentence written in a specific language is grammatically correct, or whether it is controlling the pressure in a boiler of a steam engine by deciding when and for how long to open a valve, whether it is a cardiologist diagnosing the illness of a patient by examining his ECG, or whether it is a purchase manager in a business deciding which supplier to choose to buy raw materials from.

All modern-day computers are physical incarnations of Turing's simple abstract "computing" device.

As we discover newer and newer ways of defining this set of rules and assigning an appropriate meaning to the symbols on Turing's tape, the computer will invade more and more aspects of our daily lives.

Should we be afraid of this invasion?

Why? Are we afraid of railway engines that have made travelling on foot or on horseback redundant? Are we afraid of telephones that have made shouting at the top of our voice so that our friend two blocks away can hear us, redundant? Are we afraid of the simple kitchen knife because it can cut a potato far more precisely than our nails can?

Sure that knife can also be used to stab someone in the back—but that is a choice we make. We should, therefore, be afraid of us, not the knife.

The choices we have to make to increase the power of computing and what to use it for are again ours to make.

Rumour
Books
India

www.rumourbooks.com